AFTER THE WORLD

MÁIRE BROPHY

Strange Fictions Press

AFTER THE WORLD

This is a work of fiction. Names, characters, places, and incidents are either the product of the author's imagination or are used fictitiously, and any resemblance to actual persons, living or dead, business establishments, events, or locales is entirely coincidental. All rights reserved. This book, and parts thereof, may not be reproduced, scanned, or distributed in any printed or electronic form without express written permission. For information, e-mail info@vagabondagepress.com.

AFTER THE WORLD

© 2018 by MÁIRE BROPHY
ISBN: 978-1-946050-10-6

Strange Fictions Press
An imprint of Vabondage Press LLC
PO Box 3563
Apollo Beach, Florida 33572
http://www.vagabondagepress.com

First edition printed in the United States of America and the United Kingdom, May 2018

10 9 8 7 6 5 4 3 2 1

Sales of this book without the front cover may be unauthorized. If this book is coverless, it may have been reported to the publisher as unsold or destroyed, and neither the author nor the publisher may have received payment for it.

Part One:
The Cave

The world was full of bitter brightness — stinging, blinding, searing light. It shocked my head and made it hard to open my eyes. Even a small flutter of the eyelids brought in such a cacophony, like a herd of trumpeting elephants through a small room.

I was off kilter, out of step. I couldn't walk the world as I once did. Even the blessed night didn't bring complete relief. Its power was but temporarily dimmed as the scorched earth reminded me. I could see again at night, but the sights brought no comfort. The world that I knew was gone. Everything was broken.

It had been years: scavenging, subsisting, crawling, hiding. We forgot in the glory of our civilization how it was possible to survive on so little. Orcs said we would "rather die" than carry on without our place, our people, our dreams. And yet, here I was. Surviving. Surviving on the things that were even slower or stupider than me, slow and stupid as I was. I fed on them, and time.

"Time is a changer; time is a cycle. What was once will be again." I told myself this on days when I had hope.

Hope came easily then. Not often, but easily. One day I caught a rabbit. I hadn't caught a rabbit in years. I've eaten lots of rabbit, but mostly someone else did the catching. I felt like my old self — even though my old self would never have done such a thing. Such lowly work. But it made me think I was getting faster, stronger. That time and the world could change again. Later, I discovered why I caught the rabbit.

Worse than the fever I shook with was knowing that I was not recovering. The cycle of time was not offering me an upswing. If I survived, I would remain as I was, digging in the dirt and hiding from the light. It seemed like a poor prize. That's hope for you. A total bitch.

From time to time, I met others, mostly goblins, who were on the same side. My cave is inviting — a sanctuary from the burning sun. Most of the time, I frightened them away. We were all afraid. I was terrified in those moments. I knew if my bravado didn't work, I wouldn't be able to fight them off. It was only the remnants of my iron will that kept my face from showing it.

I never actually had an iron will. I just figured out early on that I could fake it by sticking with my first assertion and never allowing the arguments of others to sway me. Of course, I was wracked with self-doubt over every small decision, but it was the only way to get to make big decisions. Be sure. *Always* sure. And then it became habit; you were just sure, as you had always been. It was unfortunate that reality didn't know about my iron will. I didn't intend to be swayed by it. But it swayed me, anyway.

It was just a few weeks after the rabbit when she came, the first orc I had seen in a very long time, drawn by the cool cave. I was still very weak, living on grubs and water from the spring that still had the taste of blackness in it. Dawn was already filling the sky when she made it inside. I should have scared her off, but I could barely stand. And with the piercing light on the horizon, she had more to lose by leaving the cave than I did by letting her stay.

I'm lucky that she chose to barter with me, rather than just kill me straight out. She had salted meat and some bread. Both were past their best, but it had been so long since I had tasted anything cured or baked, it did not matter. For this, I allowed her to stay in my cave and refill her water skins. She opened the bread and handed some to me, our fingers touched briefly. The sense of the tips of her fingers on mine lingered longer than the touch. My eyes focused on the bread. It was so long since I touched someone.

We should have shared news, talked about what happened. Tried to figure out if any orcs were still out there. It could have helped us both. But I was so tired of it. It broke my heart again and again to think on it. I could live like this but not while raking over the coals of my self-doubt. Thinking on what happened was still too raw, and when I tried, in the early days, my mind skittered away from it out of self-preservation. It was even hard to look at her. Find food, drink water, stay out of the glaring light: That was all I could manage.

She, too, was damaged. Or maybe she was always like that. I liked to imagine her as a possessor of cold reason, calculating outcomes ruthlessly, and that what happened made her different. She could not talk about it either, but her aversion manifested differently than mine. She talked as if there was a future, but only a future...she seemed to ignore the present.

She spoke of a shady valley, away from the sun's glare, where mountains and caves muted the burning sun, like there were clouds in the sky again. I knew what a bitch hope was, so I didn't entertain her. It sounded like stories we told our young when they were too scared, before we had ambition. A safe place, but not of our making.

She left a few nights later. In the time she spent with me, "a shady valley" became "The Shady Valley," a thing that might be became a thing that certainly was. In a few short days, she became so certain. The act of enforced certainty reminded me of my iron will again, but then I remembered I had resolved not to think on it. I tried to dissuade her from her resolve, but if anything, my presence seemed to make her more sure. What was I but evidence that our kind would seek out these places and shelter in caves and valleys. If she kept looking, she would inevitably find her people, and all would be lost no more.

I watched her go. The night's light was bearable but terrifying in a way that night had never been before. Or maybe I had just been in my cave too long...afraid of the night, the very thought! I watched her figure move among the rocks and debris until she was out of sight. Suddenly, I felt grievously alone. It hit me like it did on the first day — so alone, so unconnected, so lost. I called out to her. I would go with her. We would find The Shady Valley together. I would not be alone. I waited for a response, but none came. Perhaps she had gone too far. She didn't hear me. Maybe she didn't want me with her. Maybe she ran when she heard my words. *If* she heard my words.

I ran out of the cave in the direction she had gone. I tried to move as fast as I could, but I tripped over stones and dead branches. My legs were not used to that kind of exertion any more. I scrambled to stay upright, pushing forward. The ground seemed to move under my feet. Everything began to move all around me. I couldn't get purchase on the ground no matter how I dug my feet in. It was as if the cave was pulling me back. I couldn't leave it. It was the last sanctuary I would have, and I would die without it. How could I do this? I would risk everything for fear of being alone. I scrabbled on the ground and tried to push through, to break the grasp it had on me. The exertion seemed gargantuan — harder than anything I had done before. My heart pounded in my ears, and my breathing became labored. It quickly went from difficult to impossible, and I couldn't catch my breath. I took in huge gulps of air, and yet my lungs ached for more. The weight of my body fought against the lightness in my head, and the world spun in all directions. I fought to hold on and managed one last gasp before I fell to the ground, out of my senses.

The banner fluttered in the air, wafting in and out of my eye line with curious leisure. A stark contrast to the frantic chaos around me. The bodies of orcs and goblins and men churned in the sea of carnage. I was part of it, but above it. I called out orders, and the sea surged forward. A sea is just droplets of water. How many can an ocean lose, before it is just a puddle? We were an ocean — an enormous wave crashing into the land clean, washing it clean, making it new. I could afford to lose some droplets. I saw the faces of orcs trampled into the ground as we pushed forward. I felt nothing. They were the price I always knew we would pay.

I came to with coarse dirt stuck to my face. I was scared to open my eyes. Even behind my lids, I could tell that it was already lightening. I knew I would not last in full light. I was too weak to withstand it. I moved my arms and pushed myself up, still with eyes closed. This was pure foolishness. If it was indeed full light, as I feared, I would barely be able to move at all. I steeled myself and opened my eyes. It was not yet dawn, although the warning glow ran ominously through the sky. Where was I? Where was the cave? I looked around; it was unfamiliar. I had been near the cave for a long time. It could have been years, or maybe just weeks or months. How could I tell anymore? Eventually, the marking of nights on the cave walls had become irrelevant, and I had stopped doing it a long time ago.

But for all that time, I had never been here. I cast around desperately to get my bearings. I didn't have time to waste; soon the sun would be in the sky, and I would be lost. I had to find shelter. In my desperation, I ran forward, hoping to find something I recognized. It was as if the wilderness had engulfed everything I knew. Perhaps I could shelter in the trees.

A few more steps, and suddenly everything made sense, like a puzzle you suddenly understand. I knew where I was. The cave was not far. I would not have to face the day.

Soon, the blistering sun hit the land, but I was in the cave. It was again as it had been. But no. Now there was something new. What was it? My thoughts: find food, drink water, survive, and something else. Something more nebulous, running away from my fingers like quicksilver. I searched and searched. I examined the cave meticulously, except for the mouth, which I would search when the night returned. Nothing had changed. It was my cave. The smell of her lingered slightly, but there was no trace of anyone else. What was it? In my frustration I started to mutter, and despite the glaring daylight outside, I found myself shouting.

"How dare you!"

A voice I had not heard in some time. I had spoken to her and others, I had even shouted at some, but I had not bellowed. I could bellow so well. It had a magic of its own. As if orders could not be disobeyed. And yet, here I was defied. Defied by this cave not letting me leave. I had fallen lowly indeed. Oh resentment, I had almost forgotten you. I remembered a time when you powered me. Everything was always someone else's fault. The terrible thing about power is that you have no one to blame but yourself. I always enjoyed blaming others. It went well with my iron will.

Something beyond survival had finally permeated my soul, and it made me laugh. I laughed and laughed and laughed. I laughed until my sides ached, and I could not breathe, and then I laughed some more. I laughed as loud as if there were no day creatures to hunt me down and slay me. I laughed as someone who could defy the world once more.

When night came again, I left the cave. This time, I didn't run. I walked. I followed the direction she went. I might see her again, or I might not. It didn't really matter. I didn't need her. I felt sure, and the surety was familiar. How long would it last?

The journey was tough but not as bad as I had feared. Nothing could be as bad as I feared. I still survived, and it was somehow refreshing to walk through new places in the cool dark. Shelter was scarce but not impossible to find. I rarely found anything as good as the cave, but when desperate, trees could be cut and bound together to make a rudimentary shelter. Of course, the trees didn't like it, but when did they do anything other than complain and gossip? Bloody trees, they never shut up. The light still burned me through the makeshift shelter in some places, but I found that I could bear it. The darkness of the cave had let me grow stronger than I'd realized. Not strong, but stronger than a creature that leeches along the ground, and strong enough to bear small bursts of the day. I remembered when the day held no fears.

I remembered. The memories came back with my increased health. They were a hard burden to bear. Some days, I could not sleep, and my past decisions taunted me and burned me far worse than the sun. If only. If only I had. The cool night brought some ease, and I remembered my people. How they grew and prospered, and I remembered that not all my decisions were wrong. I remembered their bright eyes, their growing ambitions, and how I helped them see the world in a new way. A world that could belong to them, that they could own and shape. No longer tossed around by heartless tides, victims of circumstance, victims of steel and silver — victims. Oh, the irony. It wasn't lost on me. But their shining eyes were worth remembering, for all the pain it brought me. There was glory there and redemption and truth. It was not false like my iron will. It was real and solid, like the skeleton inside a man or the pit inside a peach. The foundation of all the things we did.

Sometimes, the journey made me nostalgic; it brought me back to my youth. I had nothing then, less than nothing, really. I was a vacuum, sucking in everything around me. Did I even have thoughts back then? I was both innocent and not at all. I knew so little, but I was full of blind ambition — that sort of directionless zeal. I knew I wanted to be someone and go places, but I didn't know who that person was or where the places were. Everyone seemed so dull, somehow blunt. I felt sharp — a creature apart. I would cut through everything in my way. I would make the path.

I was a creature apart again, here on this journey. Like those early days. I was both hopeful and fearful of who I might meet. Back then, it was someone to learn from, someone to join, or someone to fight. I feared discovery, and yet I longed for it all the same. I longed for someone to look at me and know me. To see the sharpness and all I could be. As I walked on this journey, I longed for recognition too, but I knew it would be double-edged. I wanted someone to share the grief and the loss with. Someone who understood. But that would also bring disapprobation. After all, I was surely to blame.

The thought of those piercing eyes looking at me with blame stopped me in my tracks. The world began to swirl again, the way it had on the night that she left. I dropped to the ground — experience telling me I would end up there, anyway. I was still capable of learning some things. I sat on the ground and remembered the cave and my aversion to leaving it. I placed my palms flat against the dirt as I sat. I pressed my fingers into the mossy carpet. I listened. And then I heard.

"You're not welcome here. We have healed. We don't want you back."

What did the ground know? What was it but earthworms and dead trees, anyway? This is what it had come to. The ground thought it could have an opinion now. I pressed my fingers harder. The moss didn't long resist my nails, and soon the tips of my fingers were embedded in the earth.

"By daylight, you will be found and slain. We will tell. We will shout!"

This ground is seriously delusional. The sun must have gotten to it. The ground shouting, like anyone could hear. The day creatures were no better friends to the ground than me. In fact, they wouldn't even listen to the ground.

At least I was listening to you, you stupid ground.

"LEAVE!"

I dug my nails in further and clawed them. I tore out a lump with each hand. I held them in front of me — moss and soil and insects. I squeezed them, and bits fell through my fingers. Bloody sod was defying me, these days. It would be enough to make you despair, if I wasn't out the far side of that already! With bad grace, I threw the clumps of sod against the surrounding trees. Give them something to complain about! I rose to my feet and walked on. I had no interest in this ground. Rocks had better sense, anyway. Give me an angry mountain any day.

She had told me the day creatures were multiplying and expanding. I had seen little of this around the cave, but as my way sloped down into a valley, I saw it much more. Even though the night didn't belong to them yet, they were increasingly fearless. They used to be corralled even in the day, but evidence of them was everywhere. Like a canker, they festered around certain pockets, and now there was little to stop their spread. They were a disease run rife through the land, unchecked and unchallenged in the day. The night still kept them back, but for how long?

Was it really the end for orcs? I understood that if I had stayed in my cave, they would certainly have found me one day. The cave kept the sun away, but it did not offer an escape route from anything that could chase further than the sun. I would have been trapped. It was a mercy that they had not spread so far yet. I needed to find other orcs and goblins, and those few men who lived in the dark with us — creatures who cursed the sun and wanted to curtail its tyrannical power. We needed to come together again, find a place and make it defensible. We had failed to curb the day creatures, and they had decimated us already. Would they complete the task and manage to annihilate us entirely?

My way was blocked. Or rather, not sufficiently blocked. I had been walking through sloping forests and plains with lots of scrub and rocks and shitty trees — yeah you heard me! — and suddenly there was nothing. It was as if a giant hand came down and swooped them all away and stacked the dead trees at the edges. Like a ploughed field but of epic proportions. Up until now, I always felt the only good tree was a dead tree, but lately they had been hiding me from the day creatures and the sun. They didn't like it, but they couldn't run away, because they're trees. Their grumbling had become background noise. I'd even stopped telling them to shut up. Now I would miss the whining trees. How would I continue?

First, I needed shelter. It was still full night, but if I pressed on, I would not find shelter before the day. I returned to the tree line. The trees groaned to see me back — that gave me some pleasure. I made sure to scratch some bark off as I walked by. Petty mischief was always worth doing when you have the opportunity. Eventually, I found a hollow that would serve and ripped off some branches to cover it.

A cleared plain could only mean the bloody day creatures were up to new things, reaching out far beyond themselves. I wove branches together tightly to block out the sun. I may have taken more than was necessary, but it's better to be sure than to leave a tree with limbs, I always say. I covered the canopy with dead leaves — the best kind of leaves! Then I sat and pondered my problem.

As the sky began to lighten, I slipped into my shelter. The trees grumbled for a while, and I fell asleep ignoring their complaints. It felt like minutes later when my eyes flew open. What was it? The trees were quiet — for once. I didn't move. Suddenly, the trees were shouting. They were saying to look over *here* to find me. Those rotten, fetid things. I wish I'd hurt more of them. I felt all the hairs on my body stand up. They were near. Day creatures. So near. I could hear them. The noises they made, their rasping breaths, the jangling racket they made when they spoke to each other. The trees were screaming. They sounded desperate now. Desperate and frustrated. The day creatures moved away. Their voices fainter.

Poor trees. No one listens to you. Maybe if you weren't such complainers

I thought I must have slept for hours, because day creatures were always reluctant to be out when it wasn't full light, but the gaps in the canopy showed me that it wasn't dawn yet. They had grown brazen, indeed. It would not be safe to spend any time here. I needed to cross the clearing, which I was sure was of their making. I stayed curled in my shelter as the day came in all its blazing fury, but I could not rest. The early morning interlopers were not the only creatures I heard that day. More came. Who knows why? The things they did, when not killing, have always been a mystery to me. At least killing was something I understood.

They stood around the trees, lisping and honking at each other. I wondered what they could possibly be doing. Then I remembered how many trees I had scratched. I had advertised my presence. They would know my mark. They would know I was here. I felt damp sweat prickle my skin. I shut my eyes and curled tighter into a ball. I had never felt so helpless, cowering with my arms wrapped around my knees, holding them tightly to my chest. Even our young didn't behave like this. Although those that still existed probably did now. Many of those that died had probably cowered this way too.

More honking. The trees were yelling too, but they were not heard. I was actually glad the trees were shouting — without that racket, the creatures might have heard my heartbeat. It clanged so loudly in my chest, it seemed impossible that they would not find me. But few of the day creatures are listeners. I was glad of that fact before, and I was glad of it again. They didn't listen to the ground. They didn't listen to the trees. They didn't listen to my panicky breath or my pounding heart.

I didn't think I would sleep at all that day. The panic I felt ebbed and flowed like a tide. I would calm and then I would hear them somewhere in the distance, and panic would rise up inside me again. I would hold my breath and then nothing. It was so draining, I eventually fell asleep. My sleep was fitful, and I woke up with a start. It was full night.

I pushed the cover off my shelter and looked around. The tracks showed how close they had come to me. So close. A few more steps, and they would likely have fallen over me. I felt the panic rise again, but I stopped it in time. I didn't know how much night there was left, but I had to move. I made my way back to the cleared plain, watching for any movement. They were now alerted to my presence and may have posted a sentry.

I wasn't wrong. These idiots can't see too well at night, but they often try anyway. They light giant torches in an effort to mimic their horrific sun, but it usually just serves to blind them further. At the tree line, I could see these markers in the distance. I dropped down low and sniffed the air. The wind was in my favor, and I could sense them.

In my bolder days, I would have attacked, but now I just wanted to get past them. Who knew how many there were, and I was alone. I hoped the dark would cover me as I moved through the clearing. At first I went quickly, covering as much ground as I could. The ground was churned and crumbled. It crunched under my feet, as if I was breaking a crisp seal with each step. With a start, I realized I was leaving clear tracks. This land was impossible to cross without marking. It would slow my speed to a crawl if I tried to remove the marks I was leaving. I briefly created a couple of false trails and backtracked; it was too dangerous and exposed to do more. I ran on, skipping over the ground as much as I could while bowing low.

The odor of the day creatures was growing. They had traversed this space a lot. I could see their sentry torches more clearly now, and sure enough there were figures around them. Experience told me that while I could see them, they would not be able to see me in the night. But my heart pounded all the same. I slowed and tried to make no noise — the crispy ground was no friend to me.

What was that?

Some lisping came from behind me. I had been too fixated on the torches. Some of them were stationed elsewhere. They were now on either side of me. I crept forward, my hands on the ground. Too late,

I realized I was between them and the light, and no shelter meant that they would see my shape.

An alarm sprang out, first from one of their throats and then from a bell that clanged in the night's silence. I saw bright blades raised, and one ran toward me. Out of old habit, I stood up to full height. The eager one stopped in his tracks. In that moment we both understood — if I was to die, I would surely take him with me. He wasn't one of their seasoned warriors. You could tell from his eagerness and his sudden realization that death was at hand. It was like it had never occurred to him before. This is the world of our making, a terrible legacy, when a day creature has grown to fear no death in a dark night.

He shook. I had become his whole world, but he was not all of mine. I could end all his problems in an instant, but I would still have many to contend with. An arrow punctured the ground. It was quite far away from me. They were shooting, unseeing, into the darkness, their own torches blinding them. But still, it was a problem. They could hit me by pure luck.

Only two of them could see me clearly — the child one and his companion, who was honking so loud he almost drowned out the bell. I could smell their fear. It was delicious, but I had no time to savor it. I roared and barreled into both of them, pushing them over. I ran away from the light, zigzagging in case their archers located me from the sound. I ran like I had not run in years. There was no style or grace; there was no gait. There was just desperate scrambling and the need to get away. I ran for as long as I could. Eventually I slowed, panting and gasping. I tried to listen for followers, but my breath rang in my ears, hot and hard and desperate. I looked behind me. The sentry torches were tiny dots in the distance, and my keen eyes spotted no followers. I hoped I had scared them away. But they would surely come looking in the day.

I lolloped on, sore from my burst of running but sure that I needed to be very far away come daybreak. Mercifully, the crispy ground came to an end. There was a bank of dirt and trees. Trees — I was happy to see them! The trees weren't happy to see me, and they groaned loudly in the night's wind. You'd swear I'd been the one to cut all their friends down. It's been long since they attacked any day creatures, and I'd like to point that out to them. But you can't reason with trees.

Even here there were signs of them. Their arms had stretched everywhere. I found the remains of campfires surrounded by their smell. I kept moving through the trees; I needed to keep going. The ground became rockier, sloping upward. I followed, even though I felt this would just bring me closer to the sun when it rose. I came to the crest of a hill and saw the land open up in front of me. In the distance, there was a range of high mountains. I liked the look of them; they poked the sky angrily. I liked to imagine them poking the sun.

I took a deep breath of night air in through my nostrils. I could smell the mountains in it, even from this distance. I breathed out, some of the fear going out of me with it. Mountains! Mountains, like home. Home. Don't think about it.

I regarded the plain again. Night was ending soon. Mountains might be in my future, but for now there was only this hill, and the coming nights might hold more dangers. I breathed in again, deciding the moments spent were worth the risk. I didn't have time to make a proper shelter — I had chosen distance over preparation — my best protection came from being far away from the day creatures. I walked down the hill, listening. I heard the tell-tale babble of a stream. Nostalgia again. One of the earliest things we were taught is that mud can be very useful when you are in need.

For the first time, I observed that the crispy, crumbly dirt from the cleared plain was caught in the hair on my arms. It crumbled at the gentlest of touches. Who would want that kind of dirt? Day creatures might be a curiosity to me, if they hadn't wiped out my people. I followed the sound to the stream. It was only little stream — a bit of water tumbling over some rocks. I dug my hands into the sides of the stream, and the fine silt slipped through my fingers as I pulled it out of the bank. I rubbed some on my legs, but it only left a thin film.

New problem. I need to create a mud hole to bathe in, but such a mud hole would be a beacon of my presence, if the day creatures had sent their hunters after me. I stood up and looked around. The dark was on the wane. I followed the stream back up its course and found where it merged with the trees. This ground was good and brown. A mud hole would be less obvious here. I love good brown mud...you'd think the ground would be on my side, wouldn't you?

I clawed at the edge of the stream and splashed the water over the little banks. I churned the dirt and water, scraping with my feet. The dirt and leaves started to clump together and make a paste, and I splashed more water and churned again. Before long, I had the makings of a good mud hole. If only something had died nearby, then that would be perfect.

I lay my back down into the cool mud. It squelched and farted as it clung to my skin. Oh mud, you feel so good! I rolled a little to coat those hard-to-reach places. I pulled clumps up and spread them on my arms and legs. This time, the dirt matted beautifully in my hair. I got to my knees and pushed my face into the mud, pulling it over my head and neck. It tingled all the places where the sun had burned me. How could I have forgotten how good this was? But I couldn't linger. I promised myself a long mud bath would be in my future, and I stood up and gathered leaves. I threw them over my bath, so it would be less obvious, and then I pressed as many as I could to my body before the mud dried. Then I settled myself against a large tree and pulled more leaves and tree detritus on top of me. I turned my face to the ground and fell into a deep sleep.

Stupid trees. Can't keep anything secret. They were gloating.

"He's going to find you. He's going to get you."

They woke me up with their cackling. I heard the glee in their leaves. It was night again — my time — time to go. I shook off the leaves. Despite the dying sun, some of the mud stayed on me while the top layer flaked away. I listened, blocking out the taunting of the trees. I heard nothing, so I breathed the air in through my nose. The trees were subject to the wind, same as me. They can stand against it, but they cannot change it. It brought me more than they would tell me. Day creatures! If they were chasing me, it must be warriors, not the scared younglings of the plain. I knew their warriors. I had come to fear them. A gust of wind brought me more news. They were three strong at least. The gloating trees told me they were somewhere in there. Although trees gossip so speedily, it was not clear how near they were. Near enough to smell. The trees said "he," so one of them stood out. Trees are pretty stupid, so what did that mean?

I could move while I pondered the problem. Away was better than here, so I headed down the hill again and faced the journey to the mountains. At least this wasn't like the clearing; there was plenty of cover. I walked in the stream for a bit to mask my tracks and scent. Splishy splashy lovely cool feet. Of all the times to revert to feeling like a cub. If this is madness, it has its upsides. The water tugged at the mud caking my legs. My fingers skated the surface, sometimes dipping to get in on the fun. The chill breeze swirled around my wet ankles, caressing them. The stream widened to a river, and I couldn't resist it any more. I dropped to my knees and pressed my face into the water. It hugged me, pulling me down into it, until I was lying flat and submersed. I was barely under, but my nose scraped the bottom. This was no great river, but it had extraordinary power. I felt alive again. After all this time, I was awake to the world. I lifted my head out of the water — the mud slid off me. I'd miss it, but it was a small price to pay for this feeling.

I am here. Still here after all this. After everything. The world is broken, but not me. Not anymore. I survived. I endured. I was stronger than the world. Stronger than all the parts that seemed so much greater than me. Stronger than those above me and those below me. I stood to my full height and stretched out. Every hair on my body stood up. I remembered what a fearsome sight I was. They had sent a warrior after me. The warrior had better pray to the sun that he wouldn't meet with me.

Part Two: The Mountain

I continued on. Now upright, less stooped. This land was weird. There was something odd about it. Was it hostile or friendly? I would like to have sat and listened for a bit, but I'd wasted a lot of time in the river already, and there were hunters on my tail. I kept moving. Maybe it would become clear, or maybe I'd be gone before it mattered. I glanced up at the mountains. I thought the nearest one greeted me favorably, although it is hard to tell with mountains.

There was something. *Goblin*, I thought. They're pretty odorous, so the faintness meant the scent was old. But it must have been after the world ended. These lands would have been teeming with goblins before, but until now I had sensed none. I walked on, and it became clear. Just one little goblin, his corpse rotted and bleached by the sun. They struck him with one of their biting blades. Would it be weird if I hugged him?

What had happened to me? Sometimes I barely knew myself. I stood there feeling affection for a dead goblin. I wouldn't have even bothered to spit on him before. But the day creatures were everywhere, and in all the time since leaving the cave, I hadn't seen any of my kind. This goblin survived when the world was torn apart but not the hunting that came after. He can't have been much of a challenge for their warriors. He was no threat to anything bigger than a dog. Okay, he might have got some of their small ones, but if their young couldn't fight off a goblin, they were certainly better off without them. Who couldn't fight off a little goblin?

Would I ever get away from the day creatures? Was there any place they hadn't infected? I was bigger and stronger than a goblin, but would I meet the same end — run down, slaughtered, and left to rot in the sun? I thought about it. An old voice in my head from long past declared it would have been better to die in battle, but the me that still lived and breathed was sure that it wasn't. Could it be that there was no good way to die? I thought of all of my people I had sent to death. Good deaths, glorious deaths, righteous deaths — or so I told them, and myself. We killed any that ran away. Don't die like this sniveling wretch; die like a warrior in battle! I had never empathized with the sniveling wretches before now. But I was getting very comfortable with these new depths. I walked on.

I walked on for nights; the journey was punctuated by days spent in shelters of debris and mud, sometimes in hollows, sometimes behind a rock, one time up a tree. You can imagine the nagging I got for that. Each night, I sniffed the air for signs of danger, but nothing alarmed me. I was getting used to the permanent scent of day creatures, but it was background here. They traveled through but didn't dwell here. Nothing to trouble me, but my mind was active again, and there were times I longed for a bit of trouble to distract it.

Since the cave, my survival mantra had been replaced with "find my people." It went round and round in my head. It kept me moving, kept me going night after night, even though my feet were rough and blistered. I felt battered by the wind, gentle as it was, and I could see scars and patches from the sunburns on my arms and legs. But I kept going because I needed to find my people. What happened after the finding, well that would be another matter.

The ground rose higher again, becoming rockier. I was getting closer to the mountains. Their odor was now flavoring the land. I spotted a cluster of boulders that formed a natural shelter and thought I was finally at a place where I could take a longer rest. There had not been any sign of the hunters since the trees taunted me about them. Perhaps they gave up or they failed to follow my trail. I felt it was time to risk a rest, or I would soon risk just collapsing one night. I pulled more cover over to the boulders and fell asleep.

It was day when I woke. I listened for the sound that had woken me. I could hear a scritching close to my ear. I grabbed the offender quickly. It was a large, juicy beetle. I munched on it and rolled over. The boulders shaded the worst of the sun, but the light still bounced between them. I was sleeping under sod and dirt, and I had been too tired to realize that it would bring crawlers with it. I lay there, tucking them into my mouth at a steady pace, their flavors bursting as I chewed. The alien sounds of the day carried on around me, and I fell back into a doze, with my mouth half full.

I woke again after dark with congealed insects on my lips and stuck in my fangs. The night was still, and the moon was glowing. I pulled myself out of the sod and stood up. Every part of me creaked. My joints cracked as I stretched. I wandered away from my sleepy hole, looking for water. The river was much larger now, and I scooped up handfuls of water into my mouth, swirling them around with the last of the insect bits. I stepped into the water. It felt good, but it didn't repeat its reviving magic again. Perhaps I was dead before and now that it had made me alive again, there was nothing left for it to do. The water eased my burns and blisters, and I took stock of myself.

I wasn't as robust as before; a diet of grubs will do that to you. My arms and legs had got very scrawny in the cave. To think I stayed there for so long, barely moving. The journey had shocked my body. It was like I had let it melt, and then I expected it to be solid again, without any notice. I climbed out of the river and lay on the grassy bank, the water spilling off me. As it slowed to a steady drip, I looked up at the moon. After a few moments, I roused myself, with the obligatory groans from my body. I crawled to the edge of the river and looked in.

The water was moving. Tiny waves knocked against each other and swirled around rocks, but the edges were more still. The moonshine dappled the water; it was bright and dark at the same time. The sparkle made me fearful, but then I remembered that the river was my friend. And so I looked.

There was my face. A long time since I had really looked at it. It looked weathered, worn, hard. My old scars made their familiar pattern, but there were new ones on top of them. Ones I don't remember getting. A broken fang, a legacy of that last battle, made my face look more lopsided, or maybe that was a trick of the running water. The result was that I was no prettier than I had been, I just looked weaker, older, used up, a husk. I still recognized my own face. I was surprised by the disappointment I felt at that. I felt different beyond recognition and found that I hoped it would affect the outside as well. But perhaps it was too much to hope for such a disguise.

I lay back down on the grass and shut my eyes. Dozing in the night, with the air on my skin. What a luxury. With every breath, I sunk deeper into the ground. Even the trees forgot I was there. And so did I.

It was happening all around me. We lost more and more. They cut through our bodies like they were wisps of air. All around me they fell, my soldiers, my fighters, my children. All the countless hours of training — the hollering, the whipping, the shouting. I taught them to fight by my own club. I raised bruises and welts and gave them their first scars. But it was not enough. Not near enough. When the first fell, I consoled myself that I had many more, and that we would outlast these weak-willed, soft things. They were raised with silk and cotton; their skin tore at the lightest of touch. They were no match for us, despite their steel.

And yet, we kept on dying. The waste of it. All those hours of training, I should have bestowed it on worthier creatures. If they were so lazy and soft, they deserved to die. Onward, I pushed them, onward! There would be no retreat. No comfort for them. I was at their back, and I would kill any that tried to flee. I cracked my whip. They would be worthy of me, or they would perish. Onward! I roared and bellowed until I was hoarse, and yet they defied me and kept on dying. Was that any way to treat their general, after all I had done for them? I raised them out of mud holes and caves and told them the world would be theirs. I gave them hope. I gave them glory. Were they really to repay me so poorly?

I roared until the sound rang in my own ears. The clouds fell back, and the sun poured in. I roared in defiance, and lost sight of all.

I woke up panting. In dreams, your thoughts are not your own, or they are, but in all the worst ways. How many times had I tried to repress that memory? That and a thousand moments like it, where a different decision would mean that I would not now be alone. It wasn't the sun that blinded me; I was already blind.

I stood up and felt my stiff joints shudder. I walked back to the boulders; another day's sleep and I would be on the move again. Suddenly I longed for my cave. Things were simple there. If I found my people, things would not be simple any more. The thought bloomed in my mind and made my steps falter. It's funny how little things can save you.

An arrow whizzed past where my head would surely have been if I had kept walking. The hunters were here.

Three of them.

I realized why the trees were wetting themselves with excitement. One was an elf. Elves are creatures of the day and night, and so they aren't hampered by the lack of sun. The others were not so gifted, but the bright moon made them able to see somewhat. Even still, they must have been crashing around looking for me, and all the while I was having a lovely sleep.

Stop sleeping! I just about dodged the next arrow and ran at top speed toward the elf. Close combat would work better for me, although they had swords and I did not. I remembered that bit a little too late. I grabbed hold of the elf and sunk my claws into his arms. His bright armor burned my hands, but I hurt him too. He squealed at my grasp.

This was no elven warlord. It was just some cub. There were these cubs everywhere — such an epidemic. I spun around, putting the elf between me and the others, just as one of them attempted to strike me with a sword. Elven armor's not bad — the sword didn't make it through. The elf kicked up with his legs and managed to get free of me. They squared off against me. The only bow was lying on the ground. I knew I was closer to them than they would like.

I bared my claws and roared, showing my fangs. I didn't need a sword to fight. I could scrape and tear and bite. I was not yet completely disarmed. They were nothing to me; I had faced much worse. I had faced their heroes, their kings, their gods — and these child things were not worthy to face me. I could see in their eyes that they knew it too. It had been a mistake to hunt me. Maybe their last mistake.

I rushed them — they had given me the advantage. I grabbed one of the day creatures and lunged at his neck with my teeth. It didn't take much to tear. They were so soft. The salty, metallic blood filled my mouth, and with a gurgling sound, he dropped to the ground, spilling more blood on the way. The elf took a swing at me again. This time, his sword contacted my back before I could react. He was no swordsman, but the elves had biting blades that hurt far more than dull steel. The pain sparkled across my back. It served the opposite of its purpose. I did not cower. I was not quelled. A horrified elven face is a very pretty thing.

At last, the other remembered she was there and lunged at me. I caught the blade in my hand. Of course, it cut me, but that was nothing. Someone who knew what they were doing would have taken my hand. But I was so sure. I reached out with my other hand for her throat, and she dropped the blade and ran. The elfling ran too.

So much for being hunted. They were probably just used to little goblins. Now I had two blades.

I picked up the body of the fallen one and dragged it to the river. I pulled off the leather armor. With loosened buckles, some of it might fit. I threw everything that might be of use to the side and stepped into the river. My blood darkened the water as it churned around me. I reached up and dragged the body on the bank into the river. It slid effortlessly down the riverbank and bobbed to and fro in the current. The river gently tugged it from me, and so I let go. The river gurgled its appreciation and speedily took it away. The body seemed appropriate thanks for all the river had done for me.

I stepped on to the bank again and knew that the dawn was coming. If they had but waited a couple of hours, it could easily have been my body in the river. The sun would have weakened and blinded me, and I would have been easy prey. Aloneness makes us vulnerable. I should move on, lest the younglings return with a bigger party. I pulled the leather jerkin over my head. It was very tight, and it creaked as I breathed. But it was better than nothing, and the pressure eased the stinging cut on my back. The leather breeches were a harder, but I ripped at them until they fit — anything to cover my skin in the sun. I pulled the sword belt around my middle and carried the other sword in hand.

I started to run on. The new leather hampered my gait. Day creatures run straighter than us, stretched out to their full height like an awkward, two-legged horse. The chest leather forced me to run straighter — I'm sure I was slower for it, but I kept going.

The inky sky was yellowing, but I thought I might have to risk exposure to the morning. I could run for a bit before the sun got too high — before its piercing gaze caught me. I ran toward the mountains, but they were still very far away. I was sweating under the leather, and I started to falter. Even in the damp of the morning, the day was stifling. I stopped and pulled the jerkin off me and scrabbled around to find some soft ground. With my arms freed, I dug my claws into the ground and hauled up as much dirt as I could. I dug and dug until the sweat ran down my back, and I could feel my skin start to burn as the sun hit it directly. I pulled back on the jerkin and got into the hole, covering myself in soil.

I could feel the sun's heat through the dirt; after all I wasn't buried that deeply. Soil fell into my mouth and nostrils as I sucked in the air. It was hard to breathe and keep out the light. This awkward balance would have to do.

I lay there, slowly baking in my soil oven, and thought about what had gone by. Brave little younglings, shocked to face a great orc, despite all the signs. That meant there was none of my kind nearby. She must not have come this way. Perhaps the cleared plain made her change course. Perhaps she was dead. Maybe there were no orcs in the mountains, even though these mountains looked as sweet as any I had ever seen. If there were orcs in the mountains, wouldn't they be harrying this land? Was I the last orc?

That thought was so unbearable that I let out a wail. This was a mistake, because it meant a mouthful of dirt and much coughing. Once again, I regretted letting her go on her own. Maybe we were the last ones. I lay there in despair for a while. Orcs are not really given to despair. We're not really ones to wallow. We usually just get on with things. That's how we survived when we were all hiding in holes; that's what made us a surprising threat to the day creatures. I would continue to be an orc. Onward!

I woke in the waning day and waited until dark before getting out of my soil pit. The leather had been pristine when I got it, apart from some bloodstains — always a nice touch. Now it was mottled from the soil, much more my style. I pulled the jerkin off with some difficulty. The cut on my back had congealed, making it stick to my skin. I yanked it, and it eventually came off with the scabs. I felt the blood flow on my back again, but I made myself busy tearing the seams so that it would fit better and allow me to run as I liked — bent with my arms trailing on the ground. When I put it back on, I was able to move like myself. I examined the steel of the blades — they were cheap and brittle. These were no swords with names, just bits of tin cut to shape with a scissors. My nails were sharper, but at least they would give me reach. Satisfied, I moved on, looking for higher ground so that I might scope out the land.

I wasn't wrong to move in the dawn light. There was a flicker of fire in the distance that told me the younglings went back and fetched their parents. Maybe there was a proper elf warrior among them, and I could have had a fight worthy of me. There's that word again. *Worthy.* What was I worthy of now? Maybe they would come and end my sorry existence, but I knew the will for survival burned strongly within me, and I would not go down without clawing every last second out of my life. I faced the mountains and moved off, running faster now, bolstered by my break at the river.

Foothills. Actual foothills, with proper rocks and everything. Between me and the mountains lay a thick bank of trees. It's hard to say how deep or far, but they danced about the nearest mountain's feet like the hem of an elf's gown. The nearest mountain rose up well above the trees. I just needed to go through this forest.

Something about the trees gave me pause. There were no sounds. I could hear no rustling of leaves or birdcalls. Broad leaves plastered the sky. Gnarled roots and branches mirrored each other, and the green of the leaves bled into the moss of the forest floor. I felt certain that there weren't even grubs digging in the ground here, and that these trees were never bare, even in the depths of winter. The darkness they provided was not homey. These trees were very quiet. They watched me with silent intensity. I would not scratch any bark here.

Not far into the forest, the canopy became so dense that the moon could no longer be seen. I walked carefully, picking up my feet over roots and being mindful not to break any branches as I went by. It took all my restraint not to trample a sapling in my path, but I had survived in this hard, new world long enough not to tempt fate. After I passed the sapling, I felt like the trees relaxed. But they remained silent, which is very unsettling in a tree.

It took me two nights of walking to get through the forest; I kept going through the darker ends of the day as well. It was slow, but I was protected from the worst of the sun. I sensed that I should not sleep here, and so when it was brightest, I simply sat on the forest floor and waited. By the end of the second night, the trees became sparser, and I came to the end of the tree line.

There was one tree past the tree line — a lonely pine standing separate. It was different from the others, in form and in spirit. Between the mountain ridges and inclines, and the shade from the trees, the sun was not much of a threat now. I knew the trees would keep intruders out. Most would not be as careful as I. I sat down beside the lonely pine and gave myself a blanket of dead needles. I had made it to the mountains. What was to come next scared me more than the sun or the greatest elf warrior could.

There were two options. Either I would find more orcs, or I wouldn't. I couldn't decide which was worse.

I woke knowing the silent forest was still keeping an eye on me. I walked across the slopes until I found ways to walk upward. I had to backtrack several times. I was new to this mountain, and there were no obvious orc trails or signs. Some must have survived all this time, so I kept looking.

Five nights of searching brought me to a path. It wasn't an orc path, although orcs may well have used it. It appeared to be the main pass through the mountains, although eaten up by the trees. Those trees weren't always here...they weren't even here that recently. The forest looked ancient, and it probably was, but I had learned a thing or two about trees in my time, and this was no ordinary forest.

Still, the trees had let me pass, and now I had this trail in front of me. I didn't need to worry about being flanked by day creatures as the trees, inadvertently, had my back. Things were looking up. I set forth on the mountain path.

The path twisted and turned about itself, but I decided to trust it, because I was tired of not trusting anything. It was steep and hard going and disappeared around rocks. It wouldn't have bothered me in my prime, but that was such a long time ago. Best not to think about it. At times, I felt like it was magical, tricking me into just wandering in circles, but somehow always upward. This mountain was harder on me than I expected. Maybe not all mountains welcome orcs. I stopped trudging and took a breath. Cliff walls flanked either side of the trail, and the twisting track meant that you could only see a short distance ahead or behind. In this moment, it was like the mountain was pressing against me. I looked up to the sky — the only way I was not walled in — and saw the stars glittering. I would have preferred clouds.

I sat down on the path and leaned against the wall. I pushed my ear against the mountainside. It was certainly feeling prickly — no one had talked to it in such a long time. I lay my hands against the mountain. It reminded me of a large troll — quick to leap to extreme emotions but longing for companionship. Sometimes, I think if a mountain could follow you home, it would. I thought of the mountain I grew up in, and in that moment, I ached for it. The longing overwhelmed me. I can only blame the influence of the mountain for this. Despite its own pain, it felt my longing, and it knew me. We were of a kind, me and this mountain. Stony, lonely and more emotional than was good for us.

After a while, I stood up, patting the rock wall as I rose. I stepped forward again on the troublesome path and kept heading upward. The path twisted again, but abruptly it changed, and I was on a ledge with quite the vista. I could see where I had come from, all the way across the plains. I could trace the river across the land and make out the expansive clearing. I could see more tilled fields and villages. I had not really appreciated how the day creatures had spread. I now saw that I had scarcely been more than a few hours from them during my whole journey. They were everywhere. Only the silent forest at the foot of the mountain deterred them.

Time to look beyond where I had been. This mountain stood out from the others in the range and seemed to be cut off by the forest that surrounded it. No wonder it was so lonely. I wondered why the forest had chosen to surround this mountain. The forest was much deeper between the mountains and would be much more difficult to travel through. You couldn't shut your eyes with these trees around, and I wasn't sure how long I could travel without sleep. But I would puzzle out this mountain first and then deal with moving on. I turned back up the path and continued to explore.

Walking was easier after I made friends with the mountain. It kept showing me things, eager for me to experience all there was to be had. Lovely as it was, some things were harder. It was rockier and harder to find food. Nothing seemed to live here. Perhaps the mountain drove everything away in bouts of eagerness and sulking. I wondered how I would cope when the day came, but somehow, I felt the mountain would provide.

I was getting weary from the climb, when the path opened and diverged up ahead. This main pathway split two ways. I was at a loss. One seemed to climb steeper than the other, but neither looked like clear, trouble-free paths. I stood for a few moments, resting and wondering if I was able for an even steeper climb, when something caught my eye. A third way revealed itself. It wasn't a clear trail, by any means, but I could see a way to climb up off the path; there seemed to be a ridge running above it. I traced the line further and saw another possible climbing route and something that looked like it might be a path much further ahead. The mountain was showing me the way.

Clambering up rocks meant my progress was much slower. I hauled myself over the second ridge and saw how it gave a clear view of the mountain pass, while providing complete cover. I realized that even when it had high traffic, this mountain pass was treacherous to travelers. I knew this was a place for orcs. I looked up again and continued my climb. Time was not my friend as I was aware that while hidden from the path, I would be very visible to the sun when it decided to rise.

I needn't have worried; the mountain was leading me somewhere. The trail ended. There were no more footholds to climb. Was I there? I asked the mountain, but it just gave me a significant look. I could see a way down but there was no further way up. I touched the steep mountainside with my fingers, and then it fell in to view. A door. Better than a door. An orc door. A door meant something inside. It meant tunnels, and caverns and mines, and darkness even during the day. It meant other orcs.

The thought filled me with excitement and dread. I pressed against the door. The rock seemed to bounce as I pressed it, and it took me by surprise when it sprung open against me. I stumbled back, lost my footing, and nearly fell off the ledge. At the apex of my stumble, I felt a breeze push me back. You see, it's good to make friends with the mountain.

The door revealed a tunnel filled with velvety darkness. I took some steps inside, and the door swung shut behind me. The darkness enveloped me. For a moment, I was lost. I had been exposed to the day for too long to see easily in such complete darkness. I bathed in the black and waited for my sight to adjust.

I stood there breathing in the heavy air of the tunnel. The opening of the door had changed the air currents, and they fought to settle back into their old pattern. A clamor of scents reached my nostrils. Amid the noise of rocks and dust were other, more unexpected scents. Signs of metallurgy, fire, and water flew up through the tunnel and danced around my head. But I was looking for more. I was looking for my people. No one had been in this tunnel for a long time, but perhaps the tunnel would lead me to them. After all, the mountain had sent me this way. I thought for a moment about the motivations of mountains and wondered if I had made the right choice. I thought about being stuck here forever with only the mountain to talk to… that didn't seem so bad.

While I was concentrating on my nose, my eyes started to come back to me. I could dimly see the walls and a bit down the tunnel. I hoped my underground sight would return to me with time, but this was still better than outside. At least I no longer needed to worry about the day. I patted the walls of the tunnel — the mountain had done well — and started forward, down the tunnel, to whatever I would find there.

Those first days inside the tunnel were uneventful in a way. But they were also fascinating to me. My first love, before power, was in the rocks — the way they dapple and flow. It was never any surprise to me that jewels live in rocks. Day creatures like the glitter they bring and pull them out of the rocks. Well, orcs and other night creatures do that too, but jewels are always more beautiful in their rightful place — in the veins of the mountain. I hugged my mountain again. This time, its thoughts were warmer and muzzier to me, but I could hear its pulse more clearly: seams of rocks, strata, running through the mountain, cross-connected in different ways. Mountains are both one thing and many things. They dig deep into the earth and thrust high into the sky. They provide us with everything we need to survive, and sometimes, we forget to love them.

The mountain took a breath and suddenly more scents were swirling around me. It was hard to catch them, but one of them was unmistakable: orc. It was old and stale, but it was there. I wondered how old it was. Dread didn't leap from the pit of my stomach, so it must be old enough. I walked on. The tunnels split and forked, but each time I followed the one where the orc scent was strongest. I knew I wouldn't actually meet another orc…the scent was somehow clean.

There were shapes in the tunnel ahead. My nose told me there was no one there, but for a moment I forgot to believe it. I stood stock-still waiting for them to make the first move, my heart pounding in my ears. You'd think I'd have learned by now not to have a standoff with a rock. I got my breath back under control and took some steps forward. Yes, it was a rock, but there was something next to it. An orc.

He was long dead. The clean smell was due to the lack of flesh. This was from before the breaking, or more probably, part of the breaking itself. I pulled at the skeleton until I could see his armor. This one had good steel. He bore the proud mark of our army, but he was very dead. The insignia of fire brought me back. *We will cleanse the world with the flames.* How naïve. As if anyone owned fire.

I sat down beside him for a talk. It's been so long since I chatted with one of my kind. It did not matter that he was dead. I'm sure I would not have listened to him when he was alive, so the experience would have been much the same. I told him about all that had happened to me since the breaking: about how I had run and hid and survived. I told him about the cave, and about her and the trees. He didn't seem all that interested. I guess it's not very eventful compared to what happened before the breaking. But then I told him about the river. I could see I had piqued his interest. Probably wondering if it would bring him back to life as well. So selfish!

I rose again, wondering what more I'd find here. Not far down the tunnel, I came across a few more. At least they weren't alone. All of them bore the fire sign. For a moment, I wondered if I could work out where I was. This was an orc home in my territory — there had been maps and plans. I don't know if it was my mind refusing to find the information, or if it's because the world was so utterly changed, but either way, I had not been able to understand where I was since the breaking. This mountain was certainly not where I came from, but the fire signs mean I must have been aware of it. It probably even had a name. I had to accept this information was lost to me, at least for now.

I continued on down the tunnel, and it opened up into a great hall. It was mostly empty with a few notable exceptions. The most obvious was the pile of orc corpses in the middle. That's how complete our defeat was. They killed my people, ransacked the halls, and removed their dead. I assumed they had dead too…orcs are nasty fighters. They probably burned them too; all I could see were the bones. The chatterbox up the tunnel probably got away from them, but not too far.

I walked around the hall and saw tunnels leading off in all directions. Was it possible that in this labyrinth they would have found every orc? If this were an orc home, there would be other rooms, living spaces, smithies in the deeper parts of the mountain. Could they all be empty? I took one of the tunnels that led downward. The deeper I went, the more chance I had of finding a living orc.

I walked on. There was more destruction — like the place had been scoured with fire. Bones and bits of armor littered the tunnel. I had to be careful where I stepped. The tunnel sloped steeply downward and twisted to follow the seams in the mountain. Here and there, it changed to steps and eventually, I came to a small room with five tunnels off it. The markings on the wall designated the living spaces, and I explored the first tunnel. It brought me to a series of rooms and a locked door. The door was barred from this side. I stood very still and listened for a moment. There was no sound behind the door. This place was more still than any part of the mountain I had yet encountered. I didn't want to look behind the door. I knew what I would find, and I could not have borne it.

I went back to choose another tunnel. Here the markings were clearer — not scorched away by fire. I chose the middle tunnel and kept walking downward. A great sadness weighed on me. All the while I had been in the cave, I thought of myself as apart. Losing everything had shattered me, but somewhere deep down, I had thought that orcs would go back to their holes and continue on as before, scraping and surviving. But here I was in the orciest of mountains, and no orcs. After the breaking, they were hunted all the way to their caves. I could see the evidence here. Every orc or goblin I scared away from the cave had probably died soon after. They were all gone, right down to the last cub. It was a fitting punishment for me that I would remain here alone.

More tunnels, more markings. They were all old. In my bones, I felt that nothing alive had been here for years. There was no one left, no one I could talk to. So I told the mountain. The mountain understood. The mountain was cut off from other mountains. It was lonely too. For a while, I stood there with my head pressed against the tunnel wall. Nothing mattered anymore. Everything was gone.

Even when I was a wretch living on grubs, I believed there were still orcs out there. It seemed like the truth was there in the pit of my stomach, a hollow, gnawing emptiness drilling through my guts. Now it was just me and the mountain.

It stayed like that for quite some time. I stood there in the deep dark with my eyes shut. Still, like every other orc in the mountain. Perhaps I would stay like this until the end took me, then I would join my kin, wherever they were. I wasn't sure I'd even be welcome after death. A day creature once told me that you reap what you sow. I cut him down. I thought it was appropriate at the time, but I finally understood that this broken world was of my making and that my punishment was to live in it.

Something nagged at my mind. It nagged for a long time before I paid attention. I assumed it was some bodily need demanding to be fulfilled. When I finally listened, I found it was a thought, a question. The mountain told me it was cut off from other mountains, but I saw the other mountains. This wasn't a single mountain, it was a range. Outside, the thick, silent forest separated them, but that did not stop mountains from talking to each other — they were ranges, connected deep into the earth.

After mulling it over for a while, I decided to ask the mountain. There was no answer. I pressed my hands and forehead against the rock and listened, deeply. I heard the breath of the mountain, the surges and waves of its strata, but it articulated nothing to me. I asked again — why was it so lonely when there were mountains so near? Nothing. No response. The mountain was not speaking to me. It wasn't just not talking. Mountains ramble away with their own business all the time, but this one was silent. The only sounds were things it could not suppress. It watched me intently but said nothing.

This was a puzzle. I felt it must mean something, but I wasn't sure what that could be. After everything I had seen that day, my mind was happy to have a distraction, and it turned the problem of the isolated mountain around and around. The trees meant something too; they surrounded this mountain. And they had started to do so after the world was destroyed. Day creatures were everywhere, but they no longer used the mountain pass, even though there were no orcs to harry them. I was being hunted, but they did not follow me to the mountain. It must mean something.

I walked back to the last junction of tunnels and read the markings again. They were the usual directions, talking about people and their living quarters, the great hall, the chief's rooms. The chief's rooms might be a place to start. If there was anything of value, it would be there.

The chief lived deeper in the mountain, usually beneath the great hall. It was said because it was the heart of the mountain, but I knew it was because it was both defensible and connected. The mountain chief had to know everything that was going on but had to keep himself clear of threats, both internal and external. If there were slayings in the great hall, there would surely be slayings here. I wondered how much day creatures knew about how orcs lived. They had found the cubs; they would surely have found everyone else.

I found the chief's rooms quickly enough. The outer door was splintered and broken. Obviously, they had tried to barricade themselves in, and it was eventually pointless. There were no orcs here now; my guess was that they were in the pile in the great hall. I pulled opened the remains of the doors and stepped inside. There was just rubble on the floor. Everything that was once a thing was now destroyed.

The second room had more in it. More rubble, but some if it looked like it might once have been furniture. In the corner was a chest lying on its side with its contents spilling out on to the floor. I could see sheaves of paper and scrolls. I righted the chest and picked up a piece of paper. It disintegrated in my hand. Some of the scrolls looked more robust, so I examined them. These were familiar. We had used many of these. The seals had been broken, but I could still see the fire emblem that was pressed into the wax. These were commands — commands from me — or at least my generals.

I would need light to read the scrolls, and time. But time was something I had in abundance. I moved into the third and final room — the chief's bedding quarters. Here, there were more scrolls. There were torches all over the tunnels, but they were all unlit. I searched for a tinderbox to make light. As I thought, the chief had ready means of making light, and soon I had two glowing torches. The shadows danced around the walls. I found them particularly grotesque, as if they were mocking all that had happened here.

I started reading. Most of it was exactly what you'd expect — orders and more orders. I tried to put them in time order, but it wasn't always possible. It started out with orders to defend the mountain adequately and to train for war. The first orders for troops were to be expected, but then orders were given to send more, younger, untrained orcs. The needs of war were great, the needs of the mountain less so. The needs of the orcs themselves were not considered at all. This orc home was slowly bled dry of all its fighting orcs, and in the end, it could not defend itself.

There is something here written by the chief. Instead of sending orcs, he asks for orcs. He says the mountain is important and must not be breached. He says they cannot defend themselves if they try to take the mountain from both sides. It's preposterous to think an orc mountain could not defend itself. Even with what I'd seen, it seemed crazy that they were listened to. Were they listened to? I had assumed the orcs in the fire armor were sent here, but maybe they fled here. Maybe this was their home, and they thought they would be safe if they returned here.

I returned to the same problem, where was I? None of the references made any sense to me. There seemed to be something about the mountain that was important to the war, or at least important to protect from the war. I tried to think. I tried to remember before the breaking, when all I seemed to do was give orders. Did I give these orders?

Mostly, I can't remember before clearly at all. Some of it comes back to me in pinprick detail, but only the personal things. Only those that I loved or hated, or loved *and* hated. Sometimes, I dream and everything is vivid and visceral — it was a marked contrast to my memory, which was glossed over with pain, making it hard to reach. And mostly I don't want to, but right now I had a puzzle to unravel, and if I could think back to my actions without feeling everything all at once, I might be able to glean something and make sense of this.

I peeled a wax seal off a scroll and rolled it between my fingers. The imprint was made with a ring. A ring I once wore on my finger. This, along with the vellum, gave weight to words held within. They would do what they were asked, or they would answer to me. The correspondence had got increasingly threatening. I wonder if it worked on the chief, or if he resisted at all. Orcs were always committed to their clans, unless they thought there was an opportunity for something better. That was the lever that I mostly used. Sometimes it was fear, but mostly I told them it was an opportunity. I painted a picture for them. I told the story of our glory, of our dominion, and they lapped it right up. Even as I beat them down, I told them that they could be great. I told them that they would be great. That I would beat them until they were great, and even then, I wouldn't stop. I would always be there pushing them further.

I didn't lie. I was still here. It's unfortunate that they were not.

I spent some time in the chief's rooms. I guess I can be chief of the mountain now, as well as the lowest foot soldier. I read all the scrolls and the scraps of paper that survived. I saw my own sign at the bottom of some of them. Part of my huge plans — small cogs in a big machine. These weren't outlier mountains, they were orc strongholds. I began to understand where I was. Though there were day creatures everywhere, these were not their lands. I was well within our borders, lands that were not troubled by day creatures for many thousands of years. No wonder the mountain wouldn't talk to me; maybe it had figured out that it was all my doing.

I sat there with my puzzle for quite some time. The sadness distracted me from my task and dragged me down uncomfortable roads. I would stay there for long periods staring at the ruins of what I had done. Everything was raw and wild. I saw the deaths of orcs — young and old — over and over again. I saw the burning of the mountains, of all the caves, all the holes and hiding places that kept us from the bright sun and made us safe. I saw orcs run out of tunnels, away from fire and smoke, to be slaughtered in the sun by elves and men and wizards and all the biting, viciousness that they could bring. But it wasn't enough.

I went down those roads for far too long. I stayed and felt everything until I could feel nothing. I had put off feeling anything for so long. But I couldn't stop them anymore; they tumbled through me without reason or restraint. I was there in the battles again and again, hearing myself push on without mercy, watching orcs and goblins tumble into the ground, stamped and scoured out of existence. Over and over again until I could feel nothing more.

Worn out, I lay on the cool ground with my eyes open. The flickering light from the torches lit the markings on the papers that lay all around me. Words swam in front of my eyes until I could see nothing at all. I stayed there until the torches burned out, and I was left in the blessed darkness once more.

Sometime later, I came to my senses. I doubted it would be the last time I was taken over by those memories. Everything seemed so unfinished. But I had my puzzle. Why was this mountain cut off? Knowing where I was would go some way to answering that. The scroll spoke of the Iret Mountains, one of the many orc homes. I couldn't recall anything special about these mountains, even though there were several Iret orcs under my command. They weren't the fiercest of fighters, but they possessed something else — a particular type of intelligence. Some of them could work magic, a skill that is very rare in orcs. Maybe that was it. Could this be a magical place?

The mountain still wasn't telling. It was disarming, like a chattering bird that goes silent. A part of me expected to be attacked. I patted the mountain, anyway. I thought it would tell me eventually, but after I had figured out most of it first. There's no point in running after a mountain. They have a way of becoming distant without ever moving that's intractable.

I took a moment to consider what I know. I was probably in one of the Iret Mountains. Not commonly known to have anything special, despite some of their orcs being magical. These mountains were deep enough in our territory to have not been considered vulnerable, but our forces were so shattered that they did not protect this part of the land at all. The day creatures scoured the lands and hunted down every one of my kind they could. They set fire to tunnels and burned the bodies. That seems to be something they would have done to all the mountains if they could. But something extra happened here. This mountain was, or believed it was, cut off from its range. On the surface silent, threatening trees surrounded the mountain, but what was happening at the roots?

I needed to figure out what was special about this mountain and explore the roots to find out what happened there. It was time to go through tunnels again. There had been no maps of the mountain in the chief's things. Of course, the chief would know his own mountain, but it was no help to me. I would follow tunnels downward.

Into the deep earth I went.

Travelling through orc spaces was both better and worse. There have been times in my life that I was alone without other orcs, but they were in places of wilderness or raiding the lands of the day creatures or elves. Sometimes, I would spy quietly alone for weeks. But these were not orc places, and so the lack of them was not strange. Here, everything was orcish. The deeper I went, the more I saw things that were orc-made. For the most part, they were broken or burnt, but occasionally there was something that survived intact. It was rending. An orc place without orcs was all wrong.

The orcs here were makers. The place was littered with bits of machinery. Most of its function was unclear to me, but sometimes there were bits I recognized. I was still looking for the forge. I wandered through tunnels, chambers, and halls with no clear sense of where I was going. I tried to move deeper into the mountain, but this wasn't always a clear path, and I started to feel like I was going in circles. I picked up a white rock; it was time to start marking where I had been.

I walked on, marking the walls each time I chose the tunnel that headed deeper into the ground. And yet, somehow, I kept looping back on myself. Each time when I thought I had chosen a different path, I would find myself again in a chamber with my telltale marks on the wall. I kept going but the marks increased, always heading downward but never getting any deeper. Out of perverseness, I headed up an incline and still found myself back in the same place. I couldn't hold it in any longer. I shouted at the mountain. It continued to ignore me. It still wouldn't talk to me. I wondered if I would be able to make it back to the other rooms, or if I would be stuck in this loop forever. Bloody mountains!

I slumped to the ground. Without my puzzle, I would be at the mercy of my memories.

"Take pity on me, Mountain, please."

For the first time in days, I felt a reaction from the mountain. Orcs don't plead very often, so that probably got its attention.

Unbidden and without warning, my mind filled with images of orcs pleading. They were begging for their lives, pleading to those that killed them, to the spirits that surrounded them, and to the mountain itself, that had always protected them. But no mercy came, not from the fire or the steel or the silver, and not from the mountain, even though the mountain heard all the cries. The mountain, which knew every one of them from cub to grown warrior, could not protect them. Fire coursed through the tunnels, mutilating and melting anything that was not destroyed entirely by the heat. The bodies of orcs fuelled the fire, and the last living orcs were caught by the smoke. Long after the fire scorched the upper levels, there were still noises from the barred room, but the mountain could not open the door.

Orcs cannot cry, at least not tears. I understood what I saw. It was not a torture device of my mind; it was what the mountain saw. I wished I could cry tears. I wanted the loss to leak out of me, to go away. For this was too much to bear, to hold inside, even for a mountain. I took pity on the mountain. This was all my doing, anyway.

At least the mountain was talking to me again. We both sat in silence for some time and then, unasked, it began to tell me the rest. The mountain had been angry. It was an orc mountain after all, and it had been one for many thousands of years. It was not quick to act. The mountain was sorry it could not protect its orcs, and the grief had given way to anger. Even with the orcs gone, the pass remained treacherous. The mountain sent unexpected rock falls and mudslides.

Howling winds pushed day creatures off its cliffs. It trapped travelers and toyed with them, forcing them in circles until it ended them.

The other mountains were displeased with this. They considered it unmountainly behavior. It seemed they considered shunning to be more mountainly behavior. I guess it's not like they could run away. So the other mountains faced away. The mountain continued to make trouble. Lots of creatures came through the pass. Some even tried to get into the tunnels, but the mountain didn't let them in. It had resolved to keep the orcs it had, holding them close as they withered away to bones.

Over time, more and more elves and day creatures came through the pass. The days were getting brighter, and it was harder and harder for the mountain to keep them away. They swarmed the mountain range oblivious to the terrain, the weather, and the unpredictability that had kept them away before. They colonized the lowlands and the plain. And they began to understand the land. But for some reason, they wanted the mountain. This mountain. When I asked why, the mountain ignored my question. It was not ready to tell me.

I had for some time suspected that this mountain was not ordinary, and not just because of its personality quirks. Mountain talk is often muzzy and hard to understand, but the more I talked to the mountain, the clearer its thoughts were. They rang in my ears like crystal bells. Something had changed inside this mountain; something had been brought forward by the scouring and the scorching. This was an unusual mountain. Or perhaps my loneliness was making me experience things that were not happening. Maybe the mountain was silent. I hugged the mountain, anyway. It was good to have a friend, even one that might be imaginary.

I wandered the tunnels again. I wasn't looking for anything in particular. I was mostly waiting for the mountain to tell me the rest of the story. It let me go my way now. If it was trying to keep me from something, it was doing it much more subtly. I wandered through tunnels and chambers, rooms and halls, places where orcs slept and ate and worked. Places where they kept their cubs but not the still room. I knew with certainty that I would never be ready for the still room. Much better to be where orcs lived than where they died. Sometimes I would find toys or devices, and I would tinker and play with them. These were clever orcs. They made things that were true, solid, and strong. Sometimes, I tried to rebuild smashed things. Cogs and gears would fit together with smoothness and ease, as if they wanted to be together. I would try to see the whole of the thing, to know what it was supposed to be. Mostly, it eluded me. As a leader, you're more concerned with outcomes than with mechanics. Obviously, I was bad at mechanics, as well as outcomes. But I sat and played with shafts and pulleys like a curious cub. These neat little puzzles were good tasks for me. I felt I was there in the small lives of everyday orcs. And for a time, I was comforted.

Not since the cave had I fallen into a routine. But a big orc city inside a mountain provided me with such an opportunity. I made myself a home in one of the abandoned chambers. Each day, I wandered about scavenging and discovering more about the orcs that lived there. When I tired, I would retreat to my little bed and occupy myself with an orcish toy, a scroll, or some mechanism before sleeping. All day long, I chatted with the mountain. We mostly didn't talk about anything substantial, but like a little cub, I felt the urge to tell it everything I was doing, even though it's impossible to hide from a mountain. I went such a long time without speaking that it was liberating to hear my own voice again. Sometimes, the mountain even answered me in my voice. The first time it happened, I was very concerned that I was mad, but after a while I reasoned that it probably didn't matter because I was the last orc. If I was mad, then all orcs were mad, and surely that had just become standard. It made me feel better to chatter away to the mountain. At least we had each other.

I could still smell orcs, which made me feel less alone and made it much easier to sleep. In my wanderings, I found stockpiles of food and weapons. I ignored the weapons but dug around for tasty things — more cubbish behavior. It was unlikely I would run out of food in such a place.

Then one day I found the mills. The mountain had many underground lakes and rivers. Streams ran through most places where the orcs had lived. But there was also a large cavern with a lake and several waterfalls. It was beautiful. Each stream of tumbling water had its own wheel, which attached to gears and cogs. I understood that I found the place where the work was done. This place had not been touched, and the wheels still spun in the water. So perfect was the workmanship that even though they were unattended for several years, they still spun effortlessly. The whole cavern whirred rhythmically, as the cogs and levers worked together. I sat and watched it for hours — clever orcs.

Even if I hadn't indulged this way, it was still too big to explore in one go. The machinery didn't even end in the cavern, but powered devices all through the mountain. I found several smithies and foundries for making things in all shapes and sizes. I spent hours in the one with the tiny tools — they made the most intricate contrivances. I did not really understand, but I was fascinated. Of course, there was the armory, which held the least interest. I had been very familiar with the tools of war, and they held no charms for me now. It was much more enticing to try to figure out how gears were made.

I'm still not sure if these rooms naturally held and fascinated me or if the mountain was trying to distract me and keep me away from something. I suspect it was a bit of both. As long as I was discovering their lives, the orcs would still live with me. I had begun to fear a day when the whole mountain was entirely discovered. I would no longer be able to be lost in curiosity and would have to look at the world once more — not a good prospect. So I took my time and savored it. I suppose I had the sense that I had nowhere to be, that there was nowhere to go to from here. All orc homes would be like this one, although likely they would be more completely ransacked. If I continued searching, I would likely just find more acute pain. It was easier to watch a millstone spin with no purpose, and marvel at the skill of the orcs that made it.

But I was not going to become fossilized like the other orcs here. I suppose it was inevitable that I would find it, or maybe the mountain got tired of having a secret from me. One day, I wandered past the smithies and the workshops without getting distracted. I kept on walking. Above my head, shafts and rotors clicked and whirred. I walked down a deep tunnel that was new, but warm and inviting. I followed the markings in the walls. They told me I was going to a special place, mainly by telling me that most orcs weren't allowed to go there.

I turned a corner and my path was abruptly blocked by fallen rocks. It looked impassable, so I went to take a different turn. But the mountain could not cope with the suspense anymore. Without asking, the rocks crumbled and fell to rubble at my feet. They revealed a stone door. I knew it was an important door because it had no markings. Everything about this door said "do not look here."

I touched the surface. It was smooth, unlike the walls around it, and yet it blended in. There was no handle and no obvious way of opening it. I gave the mountain a questioning look. It had removed the rocks; surely it could open the door. No response. I pressed my hands against the door and listened deeply. These orcs loved their mechanics; maybe there was a hinge or a hidden button? The door would tell me nothing. I ran my hands along the surface and then the edges. A faint line was visible where the door met the tunnel walls, but I could get no purchase in the groove.

I stood back for a moment and pondered the door. This was a part of the mountain that I could not enter. The mountain itself was not keeping me out, although it had purposefully kept others out before me. What was behind the door? I turned this question around in my mind as I walked back to the nearest smithy. None of the chief's scrolls had mentioned anything hidden in the mountain, although it was likely that anything of information had been taken. I knew of no rumors or myths about anything hidden in the Iret Mountains, despite the numbers of clever or magical orcs from there. It couldn't be a weapon, because we would have used it in the war, and if not in the war, they would surely have used it to protect themselves in those last days.

I reached the nearest smithy and looked through the tools. I needed something with a very fine edge that could get into the groove, but would also allow me enough leverage to force the door. In the end, I decided to take a number of things. There was an axe —

the most axiest of axes. Simple and unadorned, unlike a dwarf axe, but hard and deadly like an orc weapon. Good for felling trees and men, like my sire used to say. Its blade was both wide and thin. I also took one of the finer chisels, as well as a large hammer. It was a blunt tool, but I always enjoyed a bit of brute force, and it was probably worth a try.

Back at the door again, I placed the tools on the ground and regarded it one more time. I had a feeling the tools would be useless. This wasn't an ordinary door. In the absence of any other options, and in the absence of any word from the mountain, I decided to try. I tried every edge, but I could not get the axe or the chisel to fit into the groove. I pushed on the chisel until it slipped and nearly severed off a finger. Bleeding, I cursed the stupid door. I picked up the hammer and slammed it against the door. The noise boomed around the mountain, but the door did not move. This only made me angrier, and I pounded the door again and again with the hammer until the blood made the handle slip out of my hands in mid swing. I cursed the door once more.

I got the impression the mountain was laughing at me. This was a test, and I was not passing it. I turned my back to the door and sat on the ground in a sulk. The main problem with living inside a mountain is that it is hard not to hear the mountain, especially when the mountain is laughing at you. I gave the mountain a filthy look, and it stopped for a few moments. I noticed my bloody hand and went to take care of it.

I was not talking to the mountain as I walked back to the mill cavern, and I made sure the mountain knew by pointedly ignoring its remarks and cajoling. It suggested I go a certain way, and I chose the opposite. Eventually, it outfoxed me by telling me not to go into a room with running water and cloth for bandages. Outfoxed by a mountain. Would the indignity never end? I washed my hand and bound it up. Still not talking to the mountain, I headed back to my bed, where I stayed for twice as long as normal. I buried my head in the skins and continued to ignore the mountain.

By the time I finally got out of bed, my hand had almost healed. The mountain was silent. At first I assumed it was sulking. I knew

I couldn't judge on that front, but the mountain was much, much older than me, so if either of us could be excused for behaving like a cub, it should be me. But then I heard a sound, and it became clear to me that the mountain's attention was elsewhere. Several clanging and banging sounds were coming from near the great hall. I knew what they were; we'd had several in my own home. They were intruder warnings. I wondered how far they had come.

The warnings were still clanging when I got to the alarm chamber. Above the chief's rooms, but in easy reach by a connecting tunnel, the alarm chamber housed the warnings and had a view of the great hall, where most of the entrance tunnels converged. I knew that all the main entrances were collapsed, and as far as I knew, the only remaining entrance inside was the hidden one I had entered through. I don't believe I would have found it if the mountain had not showed it to me. But that doesn't mean the intruders did not have more knowledge than me. After all, someone had ransacked the chief's room. Perhaps they had even taken a map of the mountain. Maybe they had figured out how to enter by now.

I asked the mountain what was happening. It paid me no heed. So I stood there trembling in the alarm chamber. I looked down at the great hall, trying to make out the hidden entrance tunnel. Perhaps they were already inside. I tried to examine the hall to see if anything had moved. I couldn't remember how every body lay or how each of the tunnels looked. The alarms all went silent; this meant that they had passed the outer edges of the mountain. For some time, silence reigned. I couldn't think through the fog of fear.

It seemed like an eternity without sound but too quickly another alarm went off. Main entrance. Orc homes were well protected, although the brittle skeletons reminded me that this one was not protected well enough. It took me a while, but eventually I gathered myself. This was helped by the absence of an elven horde bursting into the hall. The alarm did not stop until I undid the mechanism. I knew where they were, and I needed to think without the ringing in my head.

I left the alarm chamber and went down to the great hall. I was not set upon immediately, which I took as a good sign. I walked toward the tunnel that led to the main entrance. It was still collapsed. I climbed up on the fallen rocks and got as far as I could into the tunnel. It was solidly closed. I put my ear to the rock and listened. At first there was nothing, but then in the far distance, I could hear movement. This wall of rock was solid, although not quite as solid as pure mountain. They knew enough to find the mouth of this tunnel. What else did they know?

I went back to the alarm chamber. There were no alarms, except for the rattling of the unhitched mechanism for the main entrance alarm. Well I knew where they were. But I didn't know who they were. The mountain remained unresponsive, but I got the impression it was too preoccupied with what was happening outside to care about the little orc inside. I needed more information — I needed to go outside.

I walked back up the steep tunnel to the hidden door. I even greeted my friend, who had listened to my stories. I assured him that I wasn't leaving; I was merely going outside for a little wander. He wasn't to worry. I slowly opened the springy door and was greeted by the cool night air. Just as well, because I had forgotten that it might be day. I stepped outside quickly and shut the door behind me. The sky and the land mirrored each other with stars and fires. It was as I remembered it before. I climbed down to the pathway that ran above the mountain pass. It sloped inward, so orcs might run along it in bended fashion without being seen below.

I moved slowly, listening for anything that might tell me more, and all the while fearful of the attack that might come. This secret path ran all around the mountain, but it still took me some time before I found the action. Concealing myself behind a rocky outcrop, I observed them. They weren't being quiet at all. The trees were parted and had let in a horde of day creatures — mostly men, but among them at least one wizard.

I had not seen such a group together since my last battle. The world spun again. I struggled to breathe. The tension and fear were so overwhelming that I almost wanted to run toward them to break it. I cowered back behind my rocky protection, waiting to be discovered and for the inevitable to finally happen. They would find me, and they would tear me to pieces.

Somehow, I kept on breathing and managed to open my eyes again. They were not coming after me. Not yet. I could hear the crashing sounds of metal against stone. As I suspected, they were trying to tunnel back into the mountain.

I peered over the rocky edge and realized I could actually see very little. I moved further up the path to get a better view. Those clever orcs had left several spots where guards and lookouts could view the entrance. Men and a handful of dwarves were hammering at the rocks and moving rubble out of the way. Dwarves were a bad sign: They were good tunnelers. Not as good as orcs but not bad. I watched them sweat for a while. It wasn't easy work. The wizard stood looking over them, his crumpled, green cloak flapping in the wind. All wizards are lazy bastards — you'd never catch them moving a rock. This one stood there muttering. Not a good sign.

They pulled a large rock out. I held my breath. I thought they would eventually break through, but then several rocks fell into its place. The wizard raised his muttering to a shout, and I realized who he was chanting at. He was trying to control the mountain. My lovely, unruly mountain. I understood why the mountain was preoccupied. It was fighting back. It didn't want to let these corrupters inside — these orc killers. But why did they want to come inside? They had killed all the orcs. I didn't think they were here for me. It had to be something to do with the door.

I watched them for a while longer. Despite their wizard and the dwarves, they made little progress. The mountain pushed more rocks down on them, making them more and more exasperated. Mountains are like that. You'll never have more patience than a mountain. They got careless in their annoyance and failed to take a precaution. The next rock fall caught a dwarf and a man. As they started to move the rocks to get the bodies, the wizard declared they would try again in daylight. I slipped back down the path in case their attention turned away from the fallen entrance.

Back inside the hidden entrance, I patted the walls of the tunnel. The mountain hugged me back, all our arguments forgotten. I thanked it for keeping me safe. I knew I needed to get through the door. I went back down through the great hall and the mills cavern, all the way back to the door. Everything was as I left it. The tools were lying on the ground. The blood had dried on the handle of the hammer. There was no point in trying that again.

The mountain seemed exhausted. The wizard was no pushover, and the mountain had defied him at every turn. I asked the mountain to help me again. It told me that the door would open for the chief orc of the mountain. This was not very helpful. The chief was dead. I considered dragging the orc remains down from the great hall. Perhaps one of them was the chief and the door might open if I waved his bones in front of it. I ran back up to the great hall.

Before entering the hall, I tried to listen for more tunneling noises, but my breath and heart were pounding in my ears. I took a moment to try to calm down. The piled bodies of the orcs were right in front of me. If they still had flesh, I probably wouldn't be able to find their leader, but with just bones I had no hope. I knew in that moment that I could not carry all of them down to the door. There were too many, it was too far, and the whole thing was futile anyway. Even with the right bones, the door would probably not open. This plan was all I had to go on, so I asked the mountain which one.

The response was sluggish. That wizard must be something. I asked again, *which is the chief?* The mountain managed a chuckle. It reminded me of what I had said when I found the chief's room — that I was the chief now. But the door wouldn't open for me. The mountain was gone. I hoped it would recover before the next assault, but it looked like I had to figure this out for myself. I stumbled my way back to the door, my legs complaining about the exertion all the way.

I stood in front of the door with no handles. A door that had defied whoever had killed the orcs and that would not be opened by tools or my hands. I thought about the clever orcs of this mountain, with their complex machines and puzzles. I thought I might chance it.

"Open?"

The door swung open. I couldn't help but roll my eyes. I stepped in, and the door shut firmly behind me.

Part Three: The Cavern

It was a strange room. Odd and out of place in a homely mountain. In some ways, it mirrored the mill cavern, as it had a vast ceiling and a shimmering floor. But it wasn't a lake cavern. Water didn't cover the floor uniformly, but was gathered in neat, circular pools. It looked like each pool was held in by an invisible wall or that they were just on the verge of spilling over. The liquid inside them was black, and each had a slightly different colored sheen. They pulsed in time with the heartbeat of the mountain. They were as integral to the mountain as the rock. I understood that they were magical without understanding how or what that could mean.

I walked through the pool cavern, looking for something that would explain. At the far side was another door. It was shut like the first one but opened obligingly when I issued the command. The room was a library, but it wasn't for general use. There was one table and one stool, and the rest was the home of tomes and tomes of books. Their spines covered the walls. Several were stacked on the floor, and one was open on the table. I looked at the page. It contained a message for me.

The last orc standing is chief of the mountain. I return to the fight. The losing battle, the last battle.

We are orcs of this mountain before all else. I failed because I forgot this. I let too many of our orcs go to the war. The war has come to us, but there is no one left to fight. They brought the war to us.

Whatever orcs are left in this mountain, it is your solemn charge to defend and protect this cavern from the outsiders. Let no one pass the door that does not have the blessing of the mountain.

I didn't get much further. All the accusations that I feared were here. They all knew what I had done. I couldn't decide if it were better or worse that my accusers were dead. Although if they were here, I wouldn't be surprised if they tortured me to death. I flicked through the tome. I avoided reading the more recent entries. More accusations would not help me. I needed to find out about the pools. I pulled another book out of the wall and turned the pages. They were brittle and yellowed. I needed to be careful with them. Every so often the angular scrawl changed, which I assume meant the passage of different chiefs through the mountain city. Mostly they recounted battles or conquests, but here and there were marking that I didn't understand. I changed to a different book, more of the same.

Balancing my need for speed with due deference to the orcs of the mountain who had preserved the heritage, I scoured the books for something that would help me. I found all sorts of interesting things. There were records of all the orcs born here. I knew of no other orc city where this was practiced. It meant something to be an orc from this mountain. The mountain belonged to the orcs, and the orcs belonged to the mountain. The Iret orcs have never belonged to me, no matter what I thought.

I could see from the crumbling tomes that this library had been here for many generations, but what about the pools? If they were powerful, it wasn't the kind of power that could be used to fight off the day creatures. But perhaps it was something the day creatures wanted. I returned to the pool cavern and watched them. The one nearest to me sparkled. The black water was edged with a sickly pink sheen. I peered closer, and the surface swirled as it pulsed. I reached out toward the water, and I felt an acute sense of fear.

All of a sudden, I wanted nothing to do with these pools. I wanted to get away, but I was transfixed. I couldn't pull back from the water. The pulses became more pronounced. There was no longer a gentle ripple, but the water rose and fell as if it was sprouting further with every wave. Disobeying the normal rules of water, it reached out toward me, like a fist that opened to reveal a hand with a hundred long fingers. These fingers stretched for my face; they pushed into my eyes, up my nostrils, and down my throat, coating every surface inside my head and out. I felt them spill all over my body; they coated my bones and filled every sense. I wanted to scream and scream. I have no idea if I did or not, because I knew nothing but this water that had found its way into my very marrow, coursing through every part of me, burning like molten stone. It was clear to me that soon would be my end. My body would not be able to bear this heat and pressure, and I would evaporate into nothing. The pain was all encompassing. And then, all of a sudden, it left me.

I woke with the cool, damp floor of the cavern against my face. I was surprised to still be a corporeal being after that ordeal. Indeed, I seemed to be as bodily intact as I had been before. Sitting up, I realized I was close to three pools. I wanted to be as far away from them as possible. I had no desire to experience that again. The pool that had attacked me was closest, and I slowly edged away from it. The library was the nearest escape route, but I would be trapped. The egress back into the mountain seemed much further away than I remembered. The incident was so fresh in my mind that my first sense was to get to safety. I crawled along the floor and then made a run for it. I hit the door of the library so hard, I nearly bounced off it. I fumbled and stumbled my way inside and shut it carefully and firmly behind me. I slid to the floor with my back against the door and covered my face with my hands. It seemed like things couldn't get worse. Perhaps I had died, and this was my eternity of torment for all the mistakes I had made.

Eventually, I found the strength to take my hands down from my face. I looked up at the stacks of books and paper. They sat there as before but they looked different. It seemed like my vision was tinged with the same color as the water; everything was darker but rimmed with the pink color of guts. For a while, I thought the water was still inside me, and I panicked and started scratching at my face and eyes. I did nothing but hurt myself. I tried to get my breathing under control again. When the world slowed, I could look again, and I saw that not everything was uniform. Now, certain books stood out from the others. They glowed as the water had pulsed. I gathered myself, for I had led many orcs into battle and was not one to cower on the ground in fear. Mostly.

I stood up and walked to the books, taking one of the glowing ones in hand. I had already leafed through this one before, but I saw that it was both the same book and one that was totally different. The words and markings I had read before fell into the background, and in the foreground new words and symbols glowed. Something I had not seen before. It was what I had been looking for: the story of the cavern of pools.

The Cavern of Isknaga

Long ago, when even the world was young, there was a great orc mage called Isknaga. She grew up an everyday sort of orc, was handed a club as a cub and told to go out into the world hitting things. Like all young orcs, she was told that her club was an extension of herself, and she took this quite literally. The club did as she bid it, but it wasn't always in her hands when that happened.

Orcs had no magic, and so Isknaga simply understood that her club did her bidding in the same way as her arm or her leg would. She tumbled and jostled along with the other cubs in her mountain and, despite her small size, won many fights. When the time came for the choosing of cubs to train as warriors, Isknaga held her own and was chosen to be among them.

In those times, orcs were not seen as a great threat. Great and evil wizards battled for power over all the land, and all the other creatures tried to survive without incurring their wrath. The orcs from Isknaga's mountain sometimes had skirmishes with elves, but it was mostly over small pieces of land, lakes, and rivers. Isknaga's first mission outside the mountain was to spy on the elves.

Her orders weren't exciting enough, so with the boldness of youth, she ventured further into elf territory until she found an elf camp. She watched them play with the forest, talk to the trees, and draw pictures in the air, and she understood that she shared a quality with the elves that she did not share with other orcs.

Isknaga left the mountain and went on a quest to find out everything she could about this quality, and it wasn't long before she learned of magic and of wizards. She wanted to learn how to use the gifts the spirits had given her, but no wizard would apprentice her because she was an orc, and everyone knew that orcs were not magical. The wizards were fierce and foreboding, and most would have feared to ask, but Isknaga was an orc and she was brazen as only orcs can be. She sought out every wizard she could find and asked to learn from them. They were unimpressed by her club and confused by her request. Dismayed and disillusioned, Isknaga wandered the world, wondering why the spirits had given her magic but no chance to learn about it. The spirits heard Isknaga's questions and led her gradually to the Iret Mountains.

The spirits were angry with the wizards. They had given Isknaga wizarding powers and sent her to them, but the wizards had ignored the orc and defied the spirits. The spirits cursed all the wizards that had refused Isknaga. When they died, their souls would not escape this world but come to this cavern in the Iret Mountains and impart knowledge to those that asked for it.

Isknaga had made a home in Iret, and more orcs had joined her. Their numbers grew, and a city grew throughout the mountain range. Isknaga reigned as chief of the mountain: every orc was her cub, and she looked for magic in the cubs as they grew. More than one of them had the skill — some from her line, and some from the other lines.

The wizards continued to fight with each other, but as they died, each one found its way to the cavern of Isknaga, each trapped in its own pool. She was finally able to ask them her questions, and they were compelled to answer her. But they were wizards in death as well as life, and wizards are cunning and vicious when crossed. For everything that was taught, a price was exacted. But Isknaga was as cunning as any of them, for she was an orc as well as a wizard, and more often than not, they did her bidding.

While she lived, she bade the wizards teach the young magical orcs, and much though they complained, they were forced to comply. These magical orcs helped Isknaga to build the city of Iret. Orcs would grow and flourish here, and they would be the most learned orcs. Isknaga lived longer than any orc and when she died, she became the mountain and would forever have dominion over the wizards.

After her death, the wizards became harder to manage, and only the cleverest and hardiest of orcs could get anything out of them. Only those who come to the cave with the blessing of Isknaga could leave it alive. As *you entered the cavern, Isknaga blessed you, and you were compelled to protect the orcs of Iret above all, or else she would bring her wrath upon you.*

You have faced the wizard Aklakratan to gain the knowledge to read this book. Be warned that Aklakratan was the kindest of the wizards and his demands the least severe. The other wizards exact higher prices, and since Isknaga's death, they have taken many lives and many souls.

That was the least severe price? I did not want to meet any more of these wizards. Each shimmering pool had knowledge but also a world of pain, and I was no magician. I had never had the slightest ability with magic, though I knew plenty of magic users. I understood how to use those with magic, and I understood what a powerful force it could be, but I could never master even the simplest spell. I knew who I was, unfortunately, and I knew I would be no master for these wizards. It sounded like it had been a long time since anyone had been strong enough to control them. But their mere presence would change the orcs of the mountain. That could be seen all around.

Was the mountain really Isknaga? It seemed doubtful. That was just the kind of thing orcs say in stories. And the mountain must be millennia older than her. But certainly, the Iret orcs differed from other orcs. They were no great mages, but they must have great allegiance to the clan for this to have been kept secret from me throughout the war. There were great wizards on our side too, although I suspect they were no longer in these lands. They would surely have wanted this mountain for themselves, had they known about it.

The listing of all the births was strange too. Like all creatures, orcs care for their young, but so many die when they are still very little. Orc cities usually assume there will be more orcs without counting individuals. Orc commanders count warriors, but no one counts all the orc cubs, except here. I wondered what secrets were hidden in other mountains and tunnels. Perhaps there were no typical orc homes. Iret or Isknaga still kept track of all her children. Maybe she was still looking for the great orc mage. Maybe the next Isknaga was in the still room, lost forever, along with all the other counted cubs. No wonder this was the saddest of mountains.

I took down another book that glowed with the shimmering pink. I opened the cover, and new words jumped into the foreground.

The rules of Isknaga

The cavern is a secret known only to very few orcs in Iret. Isknaga used this to bring magic to the orcs, and this magic is for orcs only. You cannot write word of this outside the cavern. If you betray Iret, with purpose or without, your soul will be lost to the mountain. Only Isknaga herself may save you, and she has not saved any.

I wondered, though, how the day creatures outside knew of this cavern. Tales of Isknaga were not uncommon among orcs, though she sometimes went by different names, Ekclanga in the North, and Eskara in my home. The stories are more or less the same: an orc mage more cunning than the world's greatest wizards who tricked their magics out of them. She gave orcs writing and made them strong. But I had never heard of this cavern, nor of the trapped souls of wizards.

Someone must have known. Perhaps this was a story told in a different way among wizards. The wizard outside must know something. I knew now what they were after, but I was no better able to protect the mountain than before. I still wasn't sure how I would get out of the cavern without being attacked again by one of the pools. This was precious, that much was certain. It was a great repository of magical knowledge, made specifically for orcs to learn — orcs that were able, that is. I doubted that I could learn anything, and I was certain that I did not want to try. The price was too high. And maybe it didn't matter anymore if there were no more orcs. What use was this library if there were no orcs left to learn from it? Maybe the wizard would just come in here and fight with the wizard pools. Maybe the dead wizards would kill the living one. That was too much to hope for. It was far more likely that the wizard outside could control these dead ones. And however much I had let the day creatures rise, I must not allow one of them to gain this magical knowledge.

First I had to get out of this room. I was chief of the mountain, and some old, dead wizards were not going to keep me locked in a library. I needed to know what the day creatures outside were doing. It might be day already, and they would restart their digging, and the wizard would return again to fight with the mountain. I stood up and flung the door open. I walked strongly and purposefully across the cavern, while making sure not to get too close to any of the pools.

The door opened and shut behind me. I touched the tunnel wall and asked the mountain how it was. The mountain was still tired but assured me it would not fail to defy the wizard. After all, what was a wizard to a mountain? I moved quickly to the alarm chamber. The main entrance warning was still clicking back and forth. This was to be expected. The intruders had camped there and believed the mountain to be empty. I wondered if there was anywhere that I could view the entrance from inside. Entrances usually have lookouts above them where rocks and boiling oil could be thrown onto intruders, but the main tunnel was collapsed and likely these lookout posts were as well.

I felt the mountain shake. They had taken up the tunneling again. It must be day. I ran down to the great hall and stood at the other side of the tunnel. Pebbles and small rocks trickled down the rubble and landed at my feet. I stood there helpless. Luckily, the mountain was not, and it fought back with a rock fall on the other side. The larger stones shifted, and more rocks fell down around me. I jumped to get out of the way. After some crashing and bouncing, the rocks settled, and everything was silent. Even the tunneling stopped. Perhaps the mountain had killed more of them.

I clambered to the top of the rubble, testing the stability as I went. This latest shift revealed one of the upper tunnels over the main entrance tunnel. I moved some of the rocks to get better access and climbed up into the gaping hole that had once been its pathway. It was half full of its own debris, so I crawled rather than ran through it. In some places, I had to shift rocks to fit through. I pulled them toward me, hoping the roof of the tunnel wouldn't come with them, and carefully pushed them behind me. I'd have to deal with them again on the way back, but they were not fixed. There was light ahead, so I knew it would not be far.

The tunnel opened out into a small lookout chamber — light fractured against the side wall. Thankfully, this was more or less stable, and the outer walls still shielded me from the sun. The views down to the tunnel below were completely obscured by rocks — I took this as a good sign. There were two outer views from this room. The room itself was hidden from all but the keenest eyes by the formation of the rocks around it. The entrance was dug into the mountain, so the lookout room jutted out over the entrance. One of the views was looking back on the entrance, the other was looking out from the mountain.

I looked at the activity around the entrance. I was much closer than my previous vantage point and could even hear them speaking. As I had seen before, there were dwarves and men, and a wizard. Serious tunneling equipment stood with them. I can only assume it was brought by the dwarves. They were not now tunneling but shifting rocks and moving bodies. The mountain had taken two more. Two of the dwarves and a man were arguing with the wizard. I guess they had not expected such an aggressive mountain. The wizard was impatient with them. I recognized the signs of one who does not like to be questioned. Unfortunately for him, he had no choice. The day creatures were arguing furiously with him. They had lost several, and he had lost nothing. In fact, he had done nothing — not lifted one rock of this worthless mountain. The wizard argued back that he had done more than they would know, and hadn't he parted the trees and got them this far into the black lands. This did nothing to quell the others. If anything, it made them more furious. What was moving a few trees and passage through a land that was now green. He promised them riches from this mountain, and all he had actually given them was pain and death. He had demanded everything and given nothing on this fool's errand. The wizard puffed himself up at these words. He told them they were the fools, that they would see, and they would be sorry.

I felt the mountain tug for my attention. It told me to watch. A fresh rock fall fell down by the entrance of the tunnel. It took them entirely by surprise, and they all had to run and jump to avoid this new threat. The man who had been arguing with the wizard failed to move fast enough, and the rocks caught him. The tunneling equipment was now buried as well. I laughed in glee, but quietly, because I didn't want them to hear me.

The wizard recovered first. He shouted at the dwarves that this was their punishment for arguing with him. I had to admire the opportunism. The dwarves were fearful. Normally, mountains were their friends. This mountain was fighting them. They could not explain what was happening. The wizard wasn't helping things by shouting at them. They didn't look as though they were fooled by him.

I took a closer look at the wizard. He seemed pretty shabby, even for a wizard. He had that hungry look that wizards get when they can smell power within their grasp. He knew about the cavern, of that I was certain. But would his lust be enough to get him into the mountain; that was a bigger question.

I watched them as the day waned. The dwarves attempted to dig out their tools, no longer arguing with the wizard. The remaining men looked uncertain. It seemed that their leader was now buried in the mountain, and they were not sure what to do. The wizard stood well back from the rubble and commanded the mountain. The mountain remained unmoved. It seemed the mountain was having an easier time now that the dwarves were not drilling. When full night fell, the wizard gave up and grudgingly lay down near their meager campfire. As he slept, the dwarves walked away unmolested through the parted trees with the remainder of their tools. The men followed them as quietly as they could. I really wanted to watch the wizard's reaction as he woke, but I too was tired. The stress had worn me out, and I felt myself falling into sleep in the cramped chamber. I roused myself, feeling that the mountain was no longer at risk. I crawled through the tunnel and back to my bed.

An alarm rang out and kept ringing. In my bleary sleep, I assumed that I must have hooked the main entrance alarm back up, but that made no sense. The alarm sound eventually made it properly into my consciousness. My eyes snapped open and my heart pounded. I leapt out of bed and ran to the lookout room. The alarm had stopped. I did not know which one had been ringing. The main entrance alarm mechanism no longer clicked side to side. Was this a new threat? Were the men and dwarves back? Maybe it was the outer perimeter alarm that marked them leaving the area. Yes, that was it. I breathed again.

I asked the mountain if everything was okay. There was no response. I touched the walls and asked again. Nothing. I put my ear to the wall and listened. I heard only the slow pulse of the rock seams, like any other mountain. I felt no other presence, heard no other thought. The panic started to rise again. Where was my mountain? I hit the wall. Still nothing. No sulks, no distraction, no games, no laughter, nothing. Silence. I cried out to the mountain. My voice broke with the overwhelming feeling of abandonment.

Another bell rang. A new sound. I looked at the marker. It was the hidden door. My hidden door. Someone had found it. They would be here soon. There was no defense left in this mountain between them and me. I ran to the mill chamber. My steps faltered repeatedly along the way. The fear and panic made me stumble. My feet pounded underneath me until my lungs ached. I thought they would burst before I made it there. I closed every door I could. Few had functional locks, but I locked and barred any that I could. Maybe I would be safe in the mill cavern; after all, it had been unharmed in the last attack. But they were looking for Isknaga's cavern, which meant they would come through here sooner or later.

I ran into one of the armories and pulled on some mail and a breast plate. My fingers fumbled with the straps. The panic made me shake all over. I grabbed a heavy sword and a shield. For the first time, I noticed the symbol on the shield was the mountain. My mountain, where were you? The alarm sound rang throughout the mountain, and then abruptly stopped. Maybe they had left — more likely they were already inside.

I dragged my shaking body to the cavern door. I had no idea if I would be protected inside without the mountain. I shouted at it to open, and it obliged. I grabbed the axe and hammer that were still outside the door and threw them inside. On second thoughts, I retrieved the chisel, as well. No sense in advertising the door.

The door slammed shut as I faced it. I dropped everything I was carrying to the floor and turned to face the cavern. Unlike the mountain, the pools seemed more awake. They pulsed more strongly than before. I didn't think I could be more scared and yet, new levels of fear kept finding me. Was it really better to be in here?

I ran to the library and looked desperately around. I could still see some books in the different colors. I grabbed at them frantically. I needed to wake the mountain or find a way to block the cavern. There had to be something. Something boomed, and the mountain shook. They were not far.

A thought occurred to me — I could ask the wizards. They were bound by the spirits to teach orcs. They would, of course, exact their price, but what else had I left to bargain with? Any power I once had was gone; my life was worth little, and my soul was already rended in a thousand pieces. All I had to offer was my guilt. That was very strong — I carried it everywhere, through all my journeys. It was there when I slept and when I woke. It was the broken world, the cleared plains, the empty mountain, the still room. It was all the orc places in the world that were now empty. It bore the weight of every orc who ever lived.

I left the library. I walked into the center of all the pools and asked out loud: "Help me. Tell me how to save the mountain."

There was no response from the pools. I steeled myself and stepped toward a pool with a yellow sheen on its black surface. It didn't respond to my presence. I held my shaking hand just above the surface, expecting every moment to be grasped and tormented. Nothing. I ran my hand through the water, and it spilled through my fingers as if there was nothing special about it.

I ran to the next pool and pushed my hands in. I waved them around under the water, all the time asking them to help me, to show me. There was no response. I called out to the mountain. It had taken pity on me when I pleaded before. But this time there was nothing. I ran between all the pools, splashing their water around and yelling, begging, pleading with them. I fell to my knees at the furthest pool. It was different, I knew somehow.

"Isknaga help me. Make them help me."

I don't know where the words came from, but deep in my bones I felt only Isknaga would help me. A voice boomed in my head. It was so loud, I couldn't hear it. There was only pain. I covered my ears, but it did nothing.

Another explosion shook the mountain. I could only feel it. The ceiling of the cavern cracked, and a spray of rubble fell down on me. My mountain, my lovely mountain, my last friend. I felt wetness on my face. I wiped with my hands and saw the blood. The voice boomed in my head again. It was very angry. I finally heard it. It said:

What have you done!

Everything was quiet, like time had stopped. I was in a new place. I could see nothing but blinding white light. The pain remained, but it was more bearable. The blood coursed down my face from my eyes and ears. It dripped onto my arms and fell beyond.

What did you do?
Where are my cubs?
You took them. You took them all.

I felt the power of her rage. Isknaga had awoken, and she had seen what I had done. I felt her reach out to her orcs and feel nothing but emptiness. A surge of pain went through me again. I choked and gasped and coughed up blood.

Greedy and grasping, you were nothing but a tool for wizards.
You took what the spirits gave you and used it against your people.

I could not respond. Everything she said was true. She grew impatient with my lack of response. My knees buckled under me. The blood clung to my face as it surged over my lip. I watched my life drain out of me, drop by drop. My head was pulled down, as if my body could no longer support it. I had long deserved to be ended, and now it would come. That thought betrayed me.

No!

You will not end now. You will go on with the torment of knowing what you did.

"The mountain?"

The words bubbled out through the blood.

You would ask something of me?

"Save the mountain."

The mountain cannot be saved. The last of them died in terror and confusion. It is gone. It is done. Nothing matters now.

"There is a wizard inside the mountain. He wants the cavern for himself."

A burst of rage again. How could I trouble her with this trifle when I had been the cause of her loss? She paused in her torment of me. I choked some breath through the blood.

This wizard is nothing. He is less than an apprentice magician. He understands nothing of the world. The cavern is safe from him. If only my orcs had been as safe from you.

I could keep you alive and torment you forever. I could show you the face of every orc that died. We will go back to the still room and watch them die.

"No. Please no."

You beg mercy? You who never showed any.

"I'm sorry. I'm so, so sorry."

The words seem so small. Not big enough to express all the guilt I felt.

Everything changed. I flew forward like the string on a crossbow, tumbling out of the whiteness and back to the dim glow of the cavern. Laughter rang in my ears. Mocking, howling laughter.

I looked up and saw a figure in the pool ahead of me. It was the shadow of a man, and it was laughing wildly.

"Oh, your guilt is so delicious. I haven't tasted anything so good in such a long time." He burst into laughter again. I was bewildered.

"I remembered Isknaga, always on about her cubs. She would be so mad at you. But she never had a true appreciation for cruelty, such a disappointment in an orc.

"You, of course, have been much more cruel in your time. But that's stale and tasteless now. Your guilt is so pungent. I could smell it when you first entered the cavern. It really overwhelms all your other flavors."

Another explosion outside rocked the cavern. The shadow in the pool shrugged.

"Wizards these days are so boring! This one has been trying to find this place for years, and it took him two days to make the mountain go to sleep."

I finally realized what had happened.

"I paid you with my guilt, so what do I get?"

"You get what you bargained for. I will show you how to cut the cavern off from others and protect it only for orcs."

"Are there other orcs left?"

"You didn't bargain for that piece of knowledge." He looked at me greedily.

"What would it cost?"

"Come back to me when you have something to offer. For now, I am satiated with your guilt. If you destroy the world again, I may feel like a second helping, but until then, you will get nothing more from me."

"How do I keep the cavern safe?"

But he was gone. The shadow had melted back into its pool.

Part Four: The Wizards

Wizards are so annoying. I've never met one that wasn't a giant pain in the arse. They're so busy being clever, they don't make any sense at all. If this one wasn't some disembodied water-soul, I'd have been perfectly happy to disembowel him. I made a new resolution to kill any wizards I met in future at the first opportunity.

He had taken the price but not given me what I paid for. I yelled at him, but the surface of the pool had returned to its shimmer, and there was no response. I cast my eyes around the cavern, but there was nothing new. Only more cracks in the ceiling and more dust falling around me. Shouting angrily, I stamped my way back to the library. I ran my eyes along all the tomes, and I was relieved to see one that looked different. This one had a blue hue.

As I opened it, new words jumped into the foreground. Many of them did not make sense to me. They talked of planes and portals, but eventually there was an instruction. There was a way to protect the cavern by hiding the mountain from all. It didn't seem too hard. All I needed to do was to read out this incantation. But finding the mountain again would be very difficult. The book contained this instruction, but the mountain would only be able to be found by someone who had been there before and knew the exact nature of the spell. I would need to take this book with me. If magical orcs remained, they would never again be able to find this place without it.

The other problem was the wizard who was trying to get into the cavern. He was inside the mountain, getting closer and closer. I couldn't kill the wizard in the pool, because he was already dead, but the other wizard was still alive and could very well do with a bit of orc vengeance.

I tucked the book under my arm, picked up the sword, and left the cavern. Magical explosions continued to shake the mountain, but I had no idea where they were coming from. I headed back to the mill cavern, occasionally dodging bits of falling debris.

Aside from the detritus from the explosions, the mill cavern remained untouched. The wizard had not even made it that far. I realized the shadow wizard might have been right — that this was not some great mage to be reckoned with. I left the main entrance to the mill cavern barred and went out through one of the smaller tunnels. Once through, I tried to cover it with the loose rocks around it. If I could keep him from the beautiful mill cavern, I would. Another explosion, but it felt further away. What was he doing?

I kept going, with my sword in one hand and the book tucked under my other arm. I needed to hide it before dealing with the wizard. I had no idea where he had got to, but I needed to draw him out of the mountain. I ran to the alarm chamber, where all of the alarms were silent. I surveyed the great hall. There was no one there now, but it was the most affected by the explosions. Rocks from the main entrance blockage had tumbled into the hall. The walls and ceiling had deep cracks, and there was a constant stream of dust and rubble falling from them.

I needed to draw the wizard out. My best chance seemed to be with the alarms. I hoped the wizard could read these simple orcish markings, but if I triggered an alarm, he might assume it was the main entrance or maybe the hidden door. Could I surprise him using the entrance guard towers or another hidden place? Perhaps I didn't need to defeat him entirely. I just needed to get him out of the mountain and then read the incantation. Maybe that would be enough.

I tugged at the alarm mechanism — it was simple enough. Unlike much of the machinery in the mill cavern, these alarms were common in most orc homes, and I knew vaguely how they were rigged. It didn't take me long to figure out how to bypass the outer sensor, and I could set it off while in the chamber. But setting the alarms off would just make the wizard investigate where the noise was coming from, which was here. I doubted I could defeat him face to face. I had probably killed a few wizards in my time, but then I had powerful magical protections gifted to me by allies. These days, I had rags and leather I stole from a day creature.

Wizards were cunning. He would see through something simple. I needed a plan. I needed it to be more than some falsely ringing alarms. I thought about what he knew. He probably didn't know I was here, or maybe he crossed paths with the cubs I fought with earlier, but the group had made no effort to hide themselves at the entrance. They assumed there was no one to contend with other than the mountain itself. It was strange that the wizard had only made it into the mountain after all the others had left. He may have known about the secret entrance but not wanted to tell the others. I briefly questioned whether it was even the wizard inside, but it was more likely that the explosions were wizard-made than anything else. Dwarves wouldn't be so careless inside a mountain.

I was standing there trying to figure out how to trick the wizard, when the main entrance alarm started clicking back and forth. There was someone out the front again. Perhaps the dwarves had returned to get their equipment or their dead. I ran back out to the great hall. I stowed the book and my sword under the pile of dead orcs. Another boom shook the mountain. A shower of rocks rained down on me, and I was stuck by something much larger than a pebble. With blood streaming down my face, I cursed the stupidity of wizards and climbed up the rubble blocking the main entrance. I scrambled up the shifting rocks until I found the tunnel to the sentry point. Pulling the rubble out of it, I squeezed through and crawled as fast as I could to the lookout station.

I pulled myself into the little room, fighting to get free of the rocks, all the while terrified I would be crushed by the crumbling mountain. The first window showed me the entrance, bathed in twilight. I could see that the rocks had shifted there too. The tunneling efforts had come to fruition now that the mountain could not respond. But mostly, it just revealed the dead bodies of the dwarves and men who were killed by the mountain. Perhaps a rock had tumbled and triggered the sensor.

I looked through the more outward-facing window and saw the problem — or at least the further problem. Another damn wizard. This one was even shabbier than the first one. Her cloak might once have been black — which made me wonder if I had known her — but I could not see her full face as she pondered the mountain.

Wizards — even when they're dead — are like a horned beetle in a goblet of ale. And here was I, alone, and faced with the problem of trying to keep two living wizards away from a cavern of dead ones. I felt a strong temptation to declare this wizard business and to just stay out of it, but then I remembered that this was the home of Isknaga, of orc magic, and the mountain itself.

The black wizard stood up. She took a deep breath and began to chant. This was not good. Some of the rocks in the entrance started to move. This was powerful magic. I doubted the black wizard would be able to keep it up for long, but perhaps for long enough. It was time for these wizards to meet each other.

I clambered back into the tunnel, still not sure if I'd make it to the end without a large rock crushing me, but somehow I made it out. My relief in the great hall was not long lived, as I could hear the black wizard's progress into the mountain. I knew she wasn't far. I could smell the air coming through the rocks.

I needed to think. I needed time. I needed to know their moves and think ten steps ahead like I used to. Panic erupted in me. It was too much. I couldn't think straight. Oh no. It was coming again. My breathing was already labored from climbing through the rocks, but it wasn't slowing even though I was still. I dropped to the ground, hoping I would stay conscious. But what was one more dead orc in this mountain?

The world came back into the focus as I lay there. There was something about the uneven floor of the hall that grounded me. I realized I was staring directly into an orc's face. He held my gaze, even though there were no eyes in the sockets. His look was reproachful, demanding.

I heard a voice, angry and comforting:

"You weasel! You lazy, dirty rat! If I catch you lying down on the job again, I'll nail you to the ground."

I sniggered to myself. He shouted this all the time, my old drill sergeant. And yet, he hardly ever nailed anyone to the ground. I heard a crack in the air and felt his whip on my back. I remembered not to flinch. We all used to wind him up, pretending we weren't scared of him, pretending his arms were too weak to mold us. He'd pummel us into fighters, whether we liked it or not, but we always pretended it wasn't working. I remember how his eyes bulged when we didn't cower. I couldn't suppress a smile.

I felt a wave of fondness for him, even as he hauled me to my feet and smacked me across the face with the handle of his whip. I giggled. He brought it back across my face in the other direction for good measure. He grabbed me by the shoulders and pulled me toward him. He yelled incoherently in my face. Flecks of spit landed on my face, and the stench of his breath — made up of ancient, rotten meat and fermented tobacco — crawled up my nose like smelling salts.

He had my attention, and he knew it.

"I gave you a job to do, soldier, and when it's done, I'll nail you to the ground myself, if you'd like!"

Of course, he was dead now. I couldn't figure out how that could be when he was here yelling in my face like old times.

I was upright and no longer gasping for air. I collected my book and sword and saluted my fallen brothers as they lay on the floor, and hurried out of the great hall, toward the secret tunnel.

The cool night wind hit my face, and the stars fluttered in the sky like flies around a campfire. I climbed down from the ledge, retracing the steps I made when I first came to the mountain. Haste made me careless, and I lost my footing more than once. Each time I fell, I wondered if it would be the end. Most of my falls were only short drops, enough to knock the wind out of me and do damage but not enough to keep me down. I fell awkwardly onto a jutting rock and heard and felt at least one of my ribs crack. I smirked at the idea that my old sergeant would consider nailing me to it, but nothing stopped me from surging forward.

I scrambled and tumbled my way down the mountainside until I saw the treeline approaching. I dug my heels in as I slid and eventually came to a stop just a few feet short of the first trees. I stood up and attempted to brush the rubble off me. Lots of it stuck to me, glued by my own blood and embedded in the cuts and grazes that were all over me. I still clenched the book, and it was mostly unharmed.

I cast around for somewhere to hide the book out of the wizards' reach. The murky forest was no friendlier. Just as they had before, my eyes were caught by the lonely pine I had slept under. It still looked benevolent to me, despite the general aggression of the other trees, and I made the decision for it to be the temporary protector of the book. I scrabbled at the roots, laid the book between them, and covered it in the needles.

I took a breath and started back up the mountainside. I was losing night, and my legs ached on my ascent. Instead of climbing back to the secret door, I made my way to the main entrance, where I hoped the black wizard would be still struggling to move the rocks. The way was hard without the mountain to help me. I could still hear muffled blasts happening inside the mountain. The surface was uneven and shifting constantly. I climbed to the mountain pass, only to find my way blocked by some newly fallen boulders. They shifted as I climbed over them. One fell and crushed my fingers. The pain was startling and then absent but returned deep and throbbing as I continued on.

Eventually, with aching legs and a throbbing hand, I came close to the entrance. I slowed to check the whereabouts of the black wizard, but there was no one there. The entrance was now clear enough for someone to walk through. Both wizards were now inside the mountain. The trees were still parted, providing a way out. For a moment, I thought about running. Maybe there was some other mountain somewhere that I could befriend.

I looked up to the summit, knelt down, and put my uninjured hand against the mountainside. I felt nothing. No hum, no thought, no pulse. Was my mountain dead and gone already?

I heard a blast in the distance, muffled by the mountain. More pebbles and rocks slid down the mountainside. A large crack appeared. They were destroying my mountain. The time to run had passed. If there was a place and time to stand and fight to the end, it was here and now. I stood up and, holding my broken fingers to my chest, I staggered into the mountain.

For the first time, I entered the Iret Mountains properly, like the lordly orc I was. Drums beat in time to announce my arrival. Animal hide stretched over wood. Thousands and thousands of them, all in time, for the coming of the great orc general. Ra-thum-thum Ra-thum-thum. They called from deep within the mountain to its peak. The beating heart. Boom-thum-thum. My standard bearers always went ahead. My personal squad flanked me. They were the deadliest orcs. I hewed them myself out of rock. Boom-thum-thum. The drumming merged with its echo. It lost its rhythm. It all merged into noise.

I entered the great hall. The noise was overwhelming. I tried to pick out the pulse again. There it was — a throbbing. It wasn't through the whole mountain, it was here. Just here.

I looked at my right hand. It was crumpled and swollen. I couldn't move my fingers. It made no sense. I looked up. I was in the great hall. There were no drums. There were no standard bearers, no chief, no squad. Just me. For a moment, there was silence. I remembered I was alone.

The floor shook, and I remembered I wasn't completely alone. It was time to deal with the wizards.

I staggered to the alarm chamber and reattached the rigged alarm. The piercing sound rang out and echoed through the mountain. I wiped the blood away from my eyes and hid myself among the dead orcs in the great hall. My vision flickered. Sometimes, I saw the hall full of living orcs, drinking, shouting, and squabbling with each other. I'd blink again, and it would be the cold, dead place I knew it to be.

Another flicker. This time something real and living entered the dead place. The green cloak with a luminous staff fluttered past my eye line. He entered the great hall first and saw the cleared entrance. He was evidently surprised, and he drew his staff before him and spun around defensively. When no attack came, he dimmed the light on his staff and examined the entrance. Maybe he thought it was the return of his friends. His shock abated, and he appeared to think again of the siren that was wailing all the while. He left the hall in the direction of the alarm chamber.

My eyes followed him out of the hall. His staff had disrupted my vision, but as it returned, I saw a shadow move. This time it wasn't a carousing, long dead orc. I wondered how long she had been there. Was she there when I hid myself under these orcs? I would have seen her, wouldn't I? The hairs on the back of my neck bristled. It was the survivalist part of me that still worked when my mind did not. I saw a blade in the dark.

The wailing stopped. The silence returned like a blanket. The shadow stopped moving. What was that about a shadow? Shadows don't move. The silence curled around me and settled over me. It pushed my eyelids shut. The survivalist was having none of this. Suddenly, the pain in my hand went from throbbing to piercing. My eyes snapped open. I looked down and saw my own left hand pulling at the broken fingers on my right. I stifled a cry. I was present again.

The light was coming again. The green wizard came back into the hall. I could see runes and insignia on the green cloak, but they were covered in dust from the mountain. It struck me that these two wizards had been on opposite sides before the breaking, and they seemed no less adversarial now. More than anything, it made me realize that in some ways, the land had returned to a time of chaos. Yes, the day creatures were everywhere, but those who hunger after power were still hungry, roving the world in search of advantage, which had presumably led both of these wizards to my lovely mountain.

The green wizard returned to the great hall with his staff. The light on it pulsed until a glob at the end floated steadily from it. The glob rose to the ceiling of the hall, still pulsing slightly. When it reached the rock, it dimmed and then burst into bright white light, making the whole hall fill with something akin to daylight. The green wizard examined the entrance again. He muttered several things to himself while doing so. Where was the black wizard? I had lost track of the shadow. The green wizard called back his glob of light, and it returned to his staff. He waved his hands over the open entrance tunnel, and for a moment, it flashed red. With greater caution, he left the great hall. I knew this time I had to follow.

I let the green wizard go ahead for several minutes. His light would make him blind, and I thought I would be able to see it quite easily from a distance. If the black wizard followed the green, I wanted to be behind her too. I wasn't sure if either knew of my existence, and I wanted to keep it that way for as long as possible.

It was very easy to follow the green wizard, for he was without grace underground. I could hear him trip and curse, despite his light, as he wandered through the tunnels. His bearings seemed no better than before, and he unknowingly doubled back on himself more than once. If he hadn't been so noisy, he might even have caught me by surprise. Even considering his clumsiness, his progress was surprisingly slow. My patience ran thin, and I let myself gain on him.

Shuffling forward silently and staying in the shadows, I eventually saw what he was doing. I found him on his knees, with one hand on the wall markings. His staff was angled under his elbow, spreading light on the book he was holding open with his other hand. He was lost, and he thought that some kind of book would show him the way.

He was very distracted, so I wondered if I could get close enough to kill him. My sword was ready. I thought about creeping forward, when he looked up abruptly. He closed his book and hid it under his cloak. I pushed back deeper into the shadows and pressed as hard as I could against the rock. The light on the end of his staff dimmed until it disappeared. I heard him whisper a new incantation, and his staff pulsed with a green light. The green light gave his face a rotten look. The light burst and scattered all over the tunnel. I felt a wave of nausea and disorientation. A new glob of green light hovered over the staff, and with another incantation, it began to move away from the wizard. It traveled down the tunnel away from me, and the wizard followed it. I let them get a little ahead, and then I followed.

The green wizard traveled with more purpose and direction this time. He was no longer lost in the upper tunnels but actually moving through the mountain. Sometimes, the glob would hover as if undecided on where to go, then it would burst and scatter and be replaced by a new glob. The new green glob would move again with renewed purpose, and the wizard followed it. My heart grew heavy with the gathering surety that he was heading toward the mill cavern.

The green wizard now walked through tunnels as if he had lived in Iret. The glob appeared increasingly certain about where it was going, and the wizard hurried along after it. He was entering clearer tunnels, so he rarely tripped.

It took several hours, but eventually he reached the entrance to the mill cavern. My gut wrenched to see that the doors were already broken open. The black wizard must already be inside. The glob didn't enter the door, and, with a gesture, the green wizard called it back to him.

At this point, I decided to stop following the green wizard and take an alternative route. I assumed that the glob was following the black wizard, and the black wizard obviously knew where she was going. I stepped back from the green wizard and chose one of the other routes into the mill cavern. I knew there was a tunnel that would allow me to view the cavern from higher up. Perhaps I could see both wizards without either of them spotting me.

The way was not as easy as I expected. Falls of rocks and stones blocked the way. Some I could climb over, and some I had to move, stone by stone. One, I had to tunnel through, squeezing my body through a large hole I made in the rubble beneath several large rocks. Eventually, I made it through to the pathway, which ran around the upper walls of the mill cavern. It had a lip that came to hip height. I squatted low and peered over the edge.

My eyes searched the cavern for the wizards. I almost let out a cry when I saw the largest of the mills was now destroyed. Water still cascaded onto the paddles, but they were pushed out of alignment, and with each turn did more damage to the mills and mechanisms beside them. At the end of that mill pool, I saw the green wizard clumsily attempting stealth. Without eyes, he made his way across the cavern, his staff stretched out in front of him, and his other hand on the lip of the pool. The water crashing into the mills and pools covered most of the noise he made.

With no obvious signs of the black wizard forthcoming, I leaned back a little and tried to take in the whole of the space. I let the roaring water and the stumblings of the green wizard become background. There was something else here that I needed to see. I waited and waited, and my heart broke again for the mountain with no pulse and was not comforted by the arrhythmic turning of the once-beautiful paddles and gears.

The cavern was vast, and the green wizard made slow progress across it. I got used to the new syncopation of the mills, and it became background like the falling water. Then I heard something different. There was something humming in the cavern. It was low and barely on the cusp of my hearing, but it was there. I searched for the source of the sound. Of course, it came from the direction of Isknaga's Cavern. I leaned out again over the ledge to see what I could see. The green wizard still fumbled in the middle of the cavern. I examined the walls through the darkness and sought the entrance to the tunnel.

Then I saw it. On the opposite side of the cavern, there was a circle of blackness more black than the darkness around it. It blocked my view utterly, and I could no longer even see the start of that tunnel. I remembered this device. It was a trick known to the dark wizards. It wasn't powerful magic but very useful. It could hide something in the dark, and it would act like a tripwire alarm. If anyone crossed it, the black wizard would know. I knew that the black wizard was near to Isknaga, and I needed to act. I felt my mouth begin to dry and then flood with saliva. I tried to calm myself. I needed to think, but my instinct was to leap over the ledge and run toward the tunnel.

Thankfully, I wasn't the only one made desperate by frustration. The green wizard got fed up with the seemingly endless stumbling and sent a pulse of green light throughout the cavern. It startled me and momentarily blinded me again. The green light faded, and a glob hung in the air over the wizard's staff. After a moment's hesitation, it found its way toward the blackened circle and hung there. The wizard hurried toward it.

I roused myself and climbed back down the passageway. It was as painful as it had been before, and I was even more hurried. At one point, I climbed through a hole in a rockfall only to have it crumble behind me. Gravel sprayed across my back as a large rock fell where I had just been. I shuddered and ran on. I lost my footing and slid and tumbled to the end of the tunnel, banging my injured hand again in the fall. Getting off the ground was difficult, and I wobbled to my feet. I took off down the opposite tunnel — I needed to take the long way to Isknaga's Cave to avoid setting off the trap.

I ran through the workshops, with rocks still falling and destroying beautiful things. I wanted to save them all, but I needed to prioritize. I slowed as I neared the end of the workshops and the tunnel to the cavern. I wasn't sure what I would find there. Or who I would find there.

As I neared the door, I saw a faint green light. There was no sign of the black wizard. The green wizard's staff had found the door. Some spell illuminated the edges, and the green wizard crouched in front of it and pondered. He flicked back and forth through his book, in between furtive glances. He knew there was someone else here. As did I. Perhaps the black wizard was already inside. He found the page he wanted and stood up.

With gravitas at odds with his tattered cloak, he began to incant. The green light grew stronger as he wove the spell, and his voice grew louder and surer. Several strands of flickering green light formed across the door. They glowed ever brighter as the spell went on. His voice reached a crescendo, and the strands of light that encircled the door ignited. I turned my head away just as the burst of light came, followed by a crashing sound and a wind of smoke I just about managed not to choke on.

I opened my eyes and turned back, but could see nothing. Smoke filled the air, and rubble puttered to the ground. Dust and dirt hung in the air and swirled into my eyes. Eventually, the smoke began to fade and the dust began to fall, and for a moment, an entirely intact door and a cursing green wizard were revealed. I stifled a chuckle but too late. It caught in my throat with the dust and the smoke.

I coughed. The green wizard spun around, staff at the ready. Before I could react, I was no longer choking from the dust and smoke but from an invisible hand around my throat. It pushed me back against the wall of the tunnel and held me there. My sword was pulled off its belt and flung down the tunnel away from me. My claws scrabbled at my throat, but I couldn't grasp anything. The wizard came toward me, holding his staff in front of him. He pinned my arms and legs to the wall but finally released my neck. I felt the fingers there long after they had left and struggled to open my throat again. The air rushed in, dust and smoke and all, and I coughed and coughed.

I coughed a little longer than I needed to. It was buying me time. The black wizard must have heard the crash of this attempt to open the door. If she was still this side of the door, things might fall in my favor.

The green wizard eyed me while I found my breath again. His face was filled with disgust. He brought his face close to mine. A little closer, and I'd be able to bite. But I was pinned, just too far away to get my teeth into him. His nostrils flared and his nose wrinkled. This one really didn't like orcs.

Here's the thing about orcs: We're not bad at heart. Well, some of us are…depending on your definition of bad. But we are all troublemakers — even the good ones, even the ones that want to play nice with the elves and the day creatures. We can't help it. We all love to stir a pot, mix it up, poke a caged wolf, poke an uncaged wolf. It really shouldn't be surprising that many orcs died because of the mischief that they made. And I was just like them. I just preferred to make mischief on a grand scale. To poke the world, caged or uncaged. So, I really think what I did next was down to my core orcishness. I pulled my head as far forward as I could, stuck my tongue out, and licked the side of the wizard's face.

He reacted with his core too. His disgust overrode all sense and suddenly, my arms and legs were free. I rushed him before he could regroup. If anyone had a right to feel disgust, it was me, not him.

He had destroyed this mountain. His errant blasts had cracked it all the way through and destroyed the clever things my orcs had made.

I barreled into him, pushing him back against the other side of the tunnel. I went for his throat with my injured hand, and with the other, I grabbed at his staff. If he came to his senses, I would not be able to defeat him. Even without his staff, he would likely be more powerful than me. I squeezed this neck, and his grip on the staff loosened. I pushed against it, and it fell to the floor and rolled away from us.

I closed my fist around his neck, but before I could end him, I felt my fingers buckle, and my hands were both pushed away. His eyes glowed green, and I was thrown backward against the other wall. The wizard stood in front of me with his hands apart. His hair swarmed around his head, and his grotesque features became exaggerated. Without touching me, he threw me across the tunnel toward the door. My back smashed into the ground, and it remembered every hardship I had put it through. He lifted me again and pinned me to the wall. He pointed to the door.

"Open it," he bellowed.

I let him sweat for a bit. No sense in encouraging this sort of behavior. I felt the pressure mount, and he pressed me harder against the wall.

"Open it!"

"There's a price."

I wasn't lying. There was a price. And he wasn't going to like paying it.

"What price?"

I smiled from ear to ear. "One more kiss"

I winked at him. Yeah, so I'm definitely an orc, even in the desperate times with nothing left, I was still willing to poke this bear.

He thrust out his arm behind him, and his staff came to his hand as if called. My arms began to feel more pressure. They were being pulled away from my body. My muscles and tendons were stretched to their limit. He was pulling my arms off, like I was an insect. My shoulder sockets were coming apart. The pain was excruciating.

I cried out. "Stop! I'll tell you!"

My arms stayed where they were, but the pressure was lessened. I could feel the parts of my arms grasp and cradle each other again.

"Open it!"

"It's not that easy."

I felt the pressure return to my arms, and the pulling started again. This time, it wasn't a steady pressure but came in intense bursts, each one yanking at my arms, pulling them out of their sockets. Between each burst, I felt both relief and dread of the next one.

"It doesn't belong to you!"

As if that would make any difference. How would that even work? The green wizard knew it didn't belong to him; he wanted to steal it. A thought occurred to me. Did he even know what he was looking for? Could I trick him with something else? My mind raced as I searched through every memory I had of the mountain.

"It's not there any more. I took it for myself."

"Open the door!"

"I told you it's not there anymore."

"I hid it in the great hall."

"Open the door!"

I felt my whole body slam against the rock.

"I wanted to take it away with me. I couldn't use it. I'm not a wizard."

Another slam for good measure. This time, the stone of the tunnel wall cracked a bone in my back, and I couldn't stop myself from roaring out. The pain seared before my mind could numb it.

"I will not stop. Open the door!"

I felt a sudden focus, perhaps brought on by the pain. Would this be the final test of my allegiance? Was there anything left I wouldn't betray?

Another slam. This time it was like it was happening in slow motion. The staff pulled my body from the wall, my arms and head lagged behind, trailing like flags, and then came the force back into the wall. It compounded the break that was already there, and my head and arms snapped back again. The impact of my head against the stone brought the world rushing back at full speed. Every feeling echoed and reverberated, and then I lost most of my senses. I didn't even feel my broken hand hitting the wall. I slumped into a heap. The green wizard was no longer holding me, and I could no longer stand.

I felt something warm on my face. I couldn't make sense of anything; it was just a cluster of sensations. It slid down my face, rolling over my lips, and falling off my chin, until only the dripping remained. I licked my lips. The taste of iron meant something.

I looked up and saw the green wizard standing over me, goggle-eyed and trying to swallow. With deadening eyes, he fell to the floor. There she was, the black wizard, standing over us both, with a bloodied knife in her hand. The shadow and the blade in the dark.

She put her arm under mine and tried to help me up. The green wizard was still gurgling on the ground. His blood pooled on the ground and arrested my eyes. She jerked me upward again and this time, I managed to get my feet under me.

"He's still alive."

I don't know why it seem important to tell her that. It didn't look like the green wizard was going anywhere other than death.

"He doesn't deserve a clean death. The longer he suffers, the greater his atonement to Iret."

I didn't expect to hear this, and the surprise finally pulled my eyes away from the blood and into the face of the black wizard. I saw her closely for the first time. Her face was hardened and bitter, and there was no mistaking her pure hatred for the green wizard. She looked at me keenly, although whether I appeared to her as an ally or a tasty morsel remained to be seen.

She moved me away from the green wizard and away from the door, back toward the workshops. We entered one, and she cleared the bench of tools and rubble and got me to lie down on it. When my back touched the bench, the searing pain came again, and this time I passed out.

It has been a long time since waking to someone's touch was anything other than alarming. She was trying to wash my wounds… but there were so many, and I was so covered in blood and dirt that she was having quite the hard time. I heard her return the cloth to the water and wring it. It seemed that while I was out, she realized the extent of this challenge. I felt a wet hand on my forehead, as if to hold it in place, and then a rag of cold water splashed down, followed by some serious scrubbing action. My poor head, after all it had been through, did it really need to be cleaned as well?

I jerked myself upward to sit up and make her stop, but I found that I couldn't really move. The effort caused another spasm in my back. She stopped scrubbing and put her hand firmly on my shoulder, indicating that I should stay down. She walked away from me. My eyes followed her as much as they could without moving my head. She had lit a fire in one of the forges. A pot steamed above it, and I watched her throw something into it. She poured the contents into a bowl and brought it to me. She helped me up slightly and put the bowl under my nose. Without meaning to, I breathed in the vapor. It had a stinging smell. I grimaced, but only for a short time, because a sensation of warmth spread through my body and dulled my brain. It didn't make me insensible. If anything, the opposite. It gave me relief from the various competing pains and that made me better able to think.

She was the first to break the silence.

"We're on the same side, you and I. There aren't many left who are."

It's not like I really expected her to be on my side. We both knew she was lying. Even when the dark wizards were allied with the orcs, there was always a tension. But there probably wasn't anything to be gained from disagreeing with her. After all, I could barely move, and I had already almost been killed by one wizard today. So I responded to her.

"Where did you fight?"

"The Agostor Valley."

"Who was your commander?"

"Lord Ter."

That shithead. I remember him well. "Did anyone else get away?"

"I don't know. Some of the orcs and goblins ran before the end. Ter was adamant we face whatever was coming, but it overpowered us."

Her face was pale as death. The words came out like a recitation rather than a story. I understood that need. I wondered if she knew who I was, but perhaps to her, I was just one orc among many. One in a sea of grunting animals. And of course, I wore no finery these days.

As she spoke, she returned to the fire to warm some water. She busied herself silently and returned to her futile task of cleaning me. I wasn't surprised that she didn't question me — she was biding her time, trying to gain my trust. She was gentler in her scrubbing this time, but no less involved. It was as if the cut in my head was a thorny puzzle to be solved and not a part of me at all. She took out her knife. With great restraint, I managed not to flinch. She started to cut my hair, and clumps mixed with dirt and blackened blood fell to the floor beside us. For some reason, I found those thuds very satisfying, but then I did have a festering head wound. She returned to washing and eventually cleaned it to her satisfaction. Then she allowed me to sit up.

"You're badly hurt."

Bloody wizards are so fond of stating the obvious as if it was something revelatory. My snappy retort was engulfed by the pain from my back.

She pulled off the mangled leather and searched my back with her fingers, pressing and prodding until I cried out. "You'll live."

I felt positively bathed in her sympathy.

She looked at me directly. "Tell me about the cavern."

"So the nursing portion of our relationship is over?"

"You're not an Iret orc."

"What makes you think that?"

"You don't have the mark. All the Iret orcs had marks on their back."

"Maybe they skipped me."

"How do you know about the cavern?"

"What cavern?"

"Sure, okay. Let's play that game. What do you want?"

"I just want to live here in peace. It's you that's trespassing."

She snorted in derision.

"I was here long before you. I was welcomed into these halls. It is you that is trespassing."

"So you must know all about the cavern then."

"There were some things the orcs here would not talk about. Even to their trusted friends."

We were leaving the pretence behind so quickly.

"And what makes you think you have a right to know now?"

"Because I want to bring our people back. We have been annihilated, and I know there is a power here that can be used for us."

"You cannot wield it. Only a magical orc can."

"Perhaps we could do it together?"

"I am not magical."

"I could teach you. And then together we can return to our former glory and make them cower before us."

I considered this. I knew she was playing me, but perhaps we could gain enough out of each other for it to be worthwhile.

"I will show you the cavern, but you must give me your word that you will teach me to use the orc power and not take it for yourself."

I saw the glint in her eye. She really did take me for a fool.

"I want only that."

She looked at me hungrily. I wondered if she thought I had never before encountered a wizard. But perhaps with her inadvertent help, I might reawaken the mountain.

After a short rest and some food, we made our way back to the door. The green wizard still lay in his pool of blood, but he still wasn't quite expired. The door opened on my command. I gestured to the black wizard to enter. She was astonished that the door opened so easily for me. She entered and I followed, the door swinging shut tightly behind us.

I let her observe the room. She stood in awe for a while and then moved into the space. I kept close to the door. The memory of those pools was still too fresh in my mind for me to be cavalier. She stepped near to a blue-hued pool. Something happened. I couldn't tell if it was just a shift in the air or the temperature of the cavern, but I knew something was there with us.

The black wizard stood by the blue pool, her attention absorbed. I waited for her to cry out in pain, but instead she laughed. Her body language changed — not to one contorted in pain, but into one that was looking to please, and be pleased. She laughed again, this time more shrill and staccato. It was like a different person standing in front of me. She spoke to the pool for some minutes, but I couldn't hear what she said. Eventually she turned to me, and simply said, "Show me the library!"

Carefully skirting the pools, I walked her to the library, and the door opened on my command. This time, I entered first and turned to look at her face as she observed the room. She was wide-eyed and excited. Without hesitation, she pulled a book from a shelf and leafed through it. She looked up at me, her face full of confusion.

"These are histories; where are the magic books?"

I realized that her talk with the blue pool had not elicited all the knowledge required. She did not know how the cavern worked.

"You must pay a price, and you must be in favor with Isknaga."

"And what is the price?"

"That is not for me to decide or exact."

This got me a withering look. I was disappointed in her.

"So soon you forget your promise. This is not for you. But for you to teach me."

"But there are no books to teach you with. I need the books."

It was time to risk it all.

"You must ask for the knowledge from the wizards in the pools to read the books. They exact a price, and it might be your life. I have spoken to two, and I do not wish to do it again unless I can control them. You must help me control them."

"I must experience this to understand."

I told her I would take her to Aklakratan, who explained how the cavern works.

We left the library and walked to the Aklakratan's pool with its sickly pink hue. I stood back and gestured to her to go forward. She moved with purpose but suddenly stopped. Watching her from behind, I could see her body tense, but she displayed none of the pain that I had endured at this wizard's hand. The tension released, and she turned away once more, moving quickly toward the library. I followed her there and saw her pick up the pink-hued book, her eyes gleaming.

"That's enough now. Time to teach me."

She waved her hand. I knew it was coming, but I was still shocked with the force of it. I was paralyzed. Stood still in the library doorway, I watched as she devoured that first book and looked up, hungry for more.

"You need to teach me."

She laughed and with a wave of her hand, she threw me out of the library and ran out herself. I was still paralyzed, lying on the floor. I had done all I could. I now relied on Isknaga. The black wizard approached the blue pool again.

This time it was different. Even though she was far away and spoke in hushed tones, I could still hear her. The wizard in the blue pool appeared this time to me too. I heard him speak to her.

"Oh lovely thing, I am so glad you decided to stay!"

She burbled again, preening as before.

"You have so much to teach me. I have found the library as you told me. Thank you."

"Oh, my dear, you won't be learning any more here."

Her expression became quizzical.

"Isknaga's curse holds sway here, above all other magic. And you have refused to teach the orc." She was alarmed. The wizard looked even more wizardly smug than usual. "But we shall have many talks. No need to talk to the others. They have no appreciation for the finer things that you and I care for."

She turned from the pool and ran toward the door. The blue pool wizard was still muttering to himself happily. I only heard snippets of "intellectual companion" and "appreciation for fine dramatic prose." She yelled at the door to open. And of course, it didn't oblige. Then she started screaming. All the horror I had expected her to experience finally came. I was released from my paralysis and got to my feet in time to watch her be dragged from the door.

The force that pulled her was unseen, but it was earthy and stronger than anything this wizard had ever encountered. She waved her arms and shouted spells, but it pulled her toward her inexorable fate without faltering. Eventually, it stopped pulling, and I watched her writhe on the floor. I almost felt sorry for her, but all my sorry was well used up.

Pinned in place on the floor but still moving, she appeared to melt. She fought hard but was somehow consumed by her own liquid self. The last I saw of her was her face — open-mouthed and wide-eyed in clawing, mute horror.

Then there was only a sloshing pool that eventually calmed to stillness.

I ran for the door, and it opened for me. The green wizard was still outside the door. Still living, as if it would be too much trouble to just die efficiently. With Isknaga's cavern door shut behind me, I stood on the green wizard's neck, crushing what was left of it. His body shuddered one last time, and then he was gone. I picked up his staff and dragged his body with me to the mill cavern. I threw his staff into the lake and dragged his body to one of the trash pits. I threw him in. I didn't have time to burn him.

And then I felt it. The last of his magic gone, I could feel my mountain waking. But it was not so simple. The mountain was in immense pain and very damaged. The dust picked up, and rocks started to move again, indicating that the waking was not going to be a quiet affair. After a brief visit to one of the armories and to one of the stores, I ran out of the mill cavern and up through the tunnels.

I had reached my living quarters when the mountain spoke to me. It understood it had been breached and violated. I stopped and stroked the wall. I told the mountain that I had a plan. I would keep it safe and allow it to heal. I was going away, and when I returned, I would do so with many orcs, some of them magical. I promised the mountain that it would be alive again in the best of ways. The mountain was too tired to argue.

I could feel rocks settling everywhere. I grabbed some tokens of my time in Iret, maps and parchments belonging to the chief, and as much food as I could carry in a satchel. I pulled on light, travelling armor and a fine woven cloak. Packed for traveling, and armed with a sword and dagger, I was ready to leave the mountain.

I scrambled through falling tunnels and made it to the great hall, where I ran out the open side that the black wizard had made. I barely made it out in time before the final collapse of that tunnel, sealing the mountain with a large crash. Stones and gravel propelled me forward, and I eventually came to rest on the ground in the dying sun of the evening.

I sat up, pulling my cloak over my head. I wasn't quite out of danger. Rocks and mud were sliding down the side of the mountain. I rose to my feet and watched my beautiful mountain crumble internally. I went to find my lonely pine.

The pine was still keeping the book safe, although it wasn't so lonely any more. The other trees now crowded it, bullying it. Well that's how it looked, anyway. I thanked the pine the best way I could — by taking the book out of its care. I returned to the main path.

The mountain was still again when I returned to its fallen mouth. I touched it and spoke to it. It replied sleepily, telling me it needed time to rest. I left my hand on the mountainside until the night turned cool. It was time to say goodbye.

I moved well back, almost to the sinister tree line, and opened the book. I looked for one last time on my mountain and read the words of the incantation. I didn't know what to expect — perhaps sparkles or lightning — but it was a remarkably quiet affair. One moment there was a mountain, and the next, it was gone. What was left was a large area, surrounded by trees.

At least the trees had the decency to look embarrassed. They were here to guard the mountain, and their purpose was gone. They switched quickly from sinister to feigned nonchalance. They had lost their purpose, but I had gained mine. My life must be spent repaying the debt I owe to all my fellow orcs. I must seek them out. Find the magic among them and bring them back to Iret. My life had meaning again.

Onward!

About the Author

Máire Brophy lives in Dublin, Ireland. By day, she works with researchers to help develop and express their ideas, and by night she mostly sleeps. In between, she's often found playing Dungeons and Dragons, eating cake, and watching movies. She is currently considering learning to play golf. Máire cohosts Irish Writers Podcast a podcast about writing — and tweets @mairebro. You can find out more information on her website mairebrophy.com. And don't worry no-one else pronounces her name correctly either.

Acknowledgements

As always I have to thank my parents and family for their support and encouragement. I am blessed with some truly fantastic friends, who have provided me with immense support and fun. That said, I have to call out a few people for their support of this book. At the forefront are my fellow writers Cathy Clarke and Kate Mulholland, without their encouragement, and precisely administered tough love, these pages would surely be blank, and I'd be trying to sell you a notebook. Most of this book was written in a period of personal upheaval, and a good lot of it was written on Hazel Moloney's kitchen table. Hazel provided more than hard surfaces — she was the first person to read the book in its draft form, and engaged with my random questions as I was writing including "are orcs mammals?" and "what do you call the armor thing that goes over the other thing." For all this, I am deeply grateful. Thanks also to Fawn and the team at Vagabondage Press for taking a chance on a new author and an orc with no name.

Made in the USA
Columbia, SC
24 June 2018